THE DEVIL'S OWN LUCK

A KENT BROTHERS NOVELLA

ELIZABETH ESSEX

All rights reserved.

No part of this publication may be sold, copied, distributed, reproduced or transmitted in any form or by any means, mechanical or digital, including photocopying and recording or by any information storage and retrieval system without the prior written permission of both the publisher, Oliver Heber Books and the author, Elizabeth Essex, except in the case of brief quotations embodied in critical articles and reviews.

PUBLISHER'S NOTE: This is a work of fiction. Names, characters, places, and incidents either are the product of the author's imagination or are used fictitiously. Any resemblance to actual persons, living or dead, business establishments, events, or locales is entirely coincidental.

Copyright © 2016 by Elizabeth Essex

THE DEVIL's OWN LUCK

Copyright © 2021 by Elizabeth Essex

Original Copyright as *"A MERRY DEVIL"*

© 2017 by Elizabeth Essex

Excerpt from ALMOST A SCANDAL

Copyright © 2019 by Elizabeth Essex

for revised edition; original copyright 2012.

All rights reserved.

All rights reserved.

Published by Oliver-Heber Books

Edited by Erica Monroe at Quillfire Author Services

Cover Design by Forever After Romance Designs

Photography by Killian Group & Shutterstock

0 9 8 7 6 5 4 3 2 1

PRAISE FOR ELIZABETH ESSEX

ALMOST A SCANDAL

"*Almost a Scandal* is a bold and brazen fast paced romance with a daring heroine and smoldering hot hero! With an explosive danger and red-hot romance this book is most definitely a book to treasure!" ~ *Publisher's Weekly*

"Essex will have readers longing to set sail alongside her daring heroine and dashing hero. This wild ride of a high seas adventure/desire-in-disguise romance has it all: nonstop action, witty repartee and deft plotting.

From the bow to the mast, from battles to ballrooms, Essex delivers another reckless bride and another read to remember." ~ *Romantic Times*

"The first book in the Reckless Brides Trilogy is a seafarer's delight. Col and Sally's high stakes adventure is fast-paced and fraught with peril. Well-timed humor punctuates the action and the use of frigate-speak adds authenticity to the shipboard dialog.

The love story teases the reader at first, as Col and Sally struggle to conceal their attraction on board the Audacious. Then things turn desperate when the circumstances of war seem intent on driving them apart. A smartly written, emotional tempest." ~ *Reader to Reader Reviews*

A BREATH OF SCANDAL

"Essex's second Reckless Bride certainly suits the title. The bold heroine easily wins readers' hearts, along with her officer and gentleman hero. Essex brings a breath of fresh and funny air to the Regency while her stylish writing and intelligent characters appeal to hearts and minds. Pure, delicious, sexy pleasure awaits readers." ~ *Romantic Times Book Reviews*

"Creating two very strong-willed characters and a mouthwatering romance, Ms. Essex has penned a deliciously compelling and heartwarming story that will keep the reader glued to the pages until the very end." ~ *Affaire de Coeur Magazine*

AFTER THE SCANDAL

"The inner growth of [the characters] coupled with the fast-paced action of the murder mystery makes this one intense, interesting adventure romance. [O]verall this is one smooth ride of a novel. Most of all, I am delighted by the turnout of this murder mystery. Elizabeth Essex has crafted a thoroughly interesting novel full of mystery, intrigue, and fascinating characters. I mean, who ever heard of a *thieving duke*?" ~ *Buried Under Romance*

"An exciting romantic tale that is guaranteed to weave a spell around you!! FANTASTICALLY WELL DONE!!!" ~ *Addicted to Romance*

A SCANDAL TO REMEMBER

"Set sail with Essex as she cleverly pits a bluestocking against a stiff-upper-lipped British naval officer and lets the sparks fly. Essex spices her fast-paced tale with fascinating details of ships and sailing and adds plenty of sexual tension, high-seas adventures, danger and desire. Readers will be on the edges of their seats reading this latest Reckless Brides tale." ~ *Romantic Times*, 4 ½ stars and TOP PICK!

"Essex's fifth Reckless Brides novel takes readers on another harrowing high seas adventure, filled from jib to mizzen with deception, sabotage, peril and surprise." ~ *Reader to Reader Reviews*

MAD FOR LOVE

"It's a fast-paced quick read that simply sparkles; the writing is deft and humorous." ~ *All About Romance*

MAD ABOUT THE MARQUESS

"This book is delightful…The dialogue is wonderful and sass wars are just about my favorite thing ever. The plot is just enough crazysauce layered on top of historical goodness. There was literally nothing about *Mad About the Marquess* that I didn't like." ~ *Smart B*tches, Trashy Books, A Review*

DEDICATION

*For my fellow maritime fiction enthusiasts,
especially those of us who read
Hornblower, or Bolitho, or Aubrey
and wondered, "Where are the women?"
To a willing foe and searoom!*

CHAPTER 1

*Aboard the French corvette **Insouciance**
Enroute to Portsmouth, England
November 2, 1811*

*T*HE FRENCH had a word for it, of course, being the French and the damned enemy, though they were only a day's sail away across the Channel.

The *coup de foudre* they called it—the stroke of lightning, the moment of force when everything changed.

Everything had changed the first moment Matthew Kent had seen *her*, the long, tall girl striding along the quay in the chilly dawn light. Though it had been more than a month ago, he remembered it as if it were that very morning—the air had crackled with charges of energy that had made it hard to breathe, his vision had sharpened and gone fuzzy at the edges all at the same time, and his legs had felt suddenly unsteady, as if he had stepped ashore for the first time in

1

weeks, instead of in days. As if he had been struck by lightning.

Love at first sight.

Which was impossible, of course.

He was Captain Matthew Kent, son of a proud, ambitious seafaring family, who had given ten and seven years to the Royal Navy—he had dodged bullets, won battles, and put damn Frenchmen to rout. He was a Post Captain of His Majesty's Royal Navy, damn his eyes, not some weak-kneed landsman who'd never seen a lass before.

But he had been strangely vulnerable to her, the long, tall clever lass—the coast of Cornwall was a devilish lonely place. And it had been a hell of a thing for a man of his caliber to be so bloody becalmed, set down in punishment for his sins by the Admiralty to sailing a fishing boat instead of a ship, when he ought to have been in command of a frigate, prowling the West Indies station like his father before him, taking corvettes and making his fortune.

But he'd always had the devil's own luck, and damned if he hadn't taken a bloody French corvette right there in Bocka Morrow, along the cliffs under Castle Keyvnor. With the lass's help he had saved the country from the threat of invasion, routed a traitor, and commanded the man responsible for the explosion that had destroyed all the munitions and materiel Napoleon had smuggled into England to provision his invading Grand Armée.

That Matthew had also, in the course of such heroism, kissed that long tall lass, was not recorded in his report to the Admiralty. The less said about her the better, because she was a smuggler, the brains behind the whole of the operation, and the Admiralty did not think highly of smugglers.

Nor could he.

No matter that he had fallen in love with her.

Devil take him, but love wouldn't reward him the way the

Admiralty would—a command was his for the asking. All he had to do was write his reports, recommend his crew for promotions, and sail the French prize back to Portsmouth for adjudication. And leave the lass behind.

But he'd always known the long, tall lass was tinder to the bonfire of his ambitions—one more spark, one more misdeed, one more kiss, and his career would go up in flames. If he didn't want to lose all he held dear—family, service, duty and honor—he had to leave her.

It was a devilish good thing he had been at sea long enough to know how to weather the storm—how to get struck by lightning and still survive.

CHAPTER 2

Village of Bocka Morrow,
Coast of Cornwall
November 3, 1811

TRESSA TEAGUE felt burnt to a cinder, as if everything inside her had been turned to ash, and all happiness had gone up in flames with the illicit cargo in Black Cove—she could almost smell the black smoke on the bitter winter wind even now, nigh on a month later, when she sat drinking tea with her mother and sister in the drafty vicarage at the top of the hill.

She ought to be happy, she really ought. It wasn't every day that one's sister became engaged to be married to a lord. And after everything her sweet sister Nessa had been through, it was only right that she finally got Captain Lord Harry Beck as her reward. After all, he was Nessa's one true love.

"Engaged!" her mother cried again and again. "And to a

lord! Nessa shall be a *lady*," she continued to remind each of them present—as if they might forget such a thing. "Such a boon, such blessedly good fortune at last."

"Good fortune that Lord Harry is also your heart's desire." Tressa kissed her sister's blushing cheek in congratulations. "I always knew if anyone could win their one true love, it would be you."

Nessa smiled, radiant with happiness. "And you?"

"Oh, no. I have no heart, so how could I ever have my heart's desire?" Tressa made her tone light and joking for her sister's sake, but the words were like a splinter driven deep into her flesh—a hurt she couldn't hope to extract without causing even more damage.

And so she would leave it be, and set her heart to turn to stone.

She would have no more of unreasoning love, which seemed a volatile, alchemical mixture of attraction, determination and happenstance, wherein the determination was more important than the attraction.

Love might not start without attraction, but it would not last without determination. If a man had none—well, there was nothing she could so about that.

She refused to be heartbroken—she refused to let any person change her own determination. If he had seen fit to sacrifice her affections on the bonfire of his ambitions, well, she had ambitions, too. And the time had come to pursue them.

But ambition for something other than a husband was unheard of in Bocka Morrow. Tressa wanted more than the limited power her mother held in their household, and she knew she would not be happy mothering up a brood of children the way her sister would. Harry was Nessa's world, and as long as they were together, whether it was a house in

Bocka Morrow, or in the captain's quarters on a ship, Nessa would be happy.

But Tressa feared that even if she were in the captain's quarters on some sea-going ship, she wouldn't be happy unless *she* were the captain. Unless she were the one in control of her own destiny.

The man, as it were, in charge.

Instead, she was the daughter of the vicar of Bocka Morrow, and as such was expected to be nothing but kindness and light. But she wasn't feeling particularly charitable. Or even Christian. In fact, she had never before had such an ardent desire to knock heads together.

Just one head in particular, though some of the others in this excuse for a village could also stand with a good shaking up.

It wasn't charity that was lacking in her world, but justice.

Yes. Being filled with righteous anger was far better than the alternative—being heartbroken. It was anger that heated her throat to a raw ache, and rage that stung, salty and hot behind her eyes.

"But I thought that you and Captain Kent…" Nessa ventured.

"No. You were wrong. I was wrong." Tressa forced herself to smile over her hurt as she drew her sister's arm through hers. "But we will speak of him no more, for it is your day, and your triumph. I will allow nothing to dim your happiness."

Nessa looked at her with a terrible combination of pity and relief but said nothing more. No one liked to say anything or contradict Tressa in any way. No one ever did.

Because Tressa Teague was different. She was *not* nice.

Not quiet or obedient or modest or anything a vicar's daughter was meant to be.

She was independent, irreverent, and unconventional.

She read Wollstonecraft and Wilberforce and *De Re Militari* by the Roman writer Publius Flavius Renatus—sneaked from her father's study when he wasn't paying attention—which was always.

She was difficult.

Everyone said so. Even Nessa, who drank so deeply of the milk of human kindness Tressa feared she would drown, would acknowledge that her younger sister was not a girl who suffered fools gladly.

And evidently, fools suffered her even less.

Because Captain Matthew Kent was a fool if he thought he could come to Bocka Morrow and charm her off her feet and leave her broken-hearted.

But leave her he did.

It was going to be a long, cold winter alone.

CHAPTER 3

Cliff House,
Falmouth, England
November 16, 1811

THE LETTER from the Admiralty arrived at his family's home on the afternoon post—in consequence of the successful action against the smugglers off the coast of Cornwall, it was the Lord High Admiral's pleasure to post Captain Matthew Kent to the West Indies, where he would take over his father's former position, and become the youngest captain ever to command that squadron.

He was once again Captain Matthew Kent in name and in posting. The advancement was a boon to his career, and a balm to his savaged pride. It really was as his father, the esteemed Captain Sir Alexander Kent had always said—"If you succeed, no question will be asked—but if you fail, no explanation will ever be enough."

No questions about Bocka Morrow and Black Cove had been asked. Not even by his family, who simply accepted his success as a forgone conclusion, and not the product of toil and worry and the devil's own luck.

And the help of one long, tall, perspicacious lass.

"I understand congratulations are in order, Matts." His brother Owen, and Owen's petite, vivacious wife Grace, greeted Matthew's late entrance into breakfast. "West Indies Squadron—quite the coup to take over from Father there."

"I am very pleased," was Matthew's measured response. It wouldn't do to blow one's own trumpet too loudly—his brothers would twit him unmercifully for anything they deemed braggartish.

"Taking a French corvette in Cornwall," Owen chuckled. "Who'd have thought it?"

The long, tall girl had thought it. Without her superior brain and attention to detail, he might still be stuck twiddling his thumbs in Bocka Morrow's harbor while Napoleon's English agent ran loose, wreaking havoc about the countryside.

Yet Matthew had not mentioned her assistance in his reports to the Admiralty. Nor had he so much as spoken Tressa Teague's name among his family.

But there, he had finally said her name—Tressa Teague, third and last daughter of Reverend Teague, vicar of Bocka Morrow. Tressa Teague, with her slanted, sleepy eyes that made her look like a cat in a sunbeam, but who was the brilliant, steady brains behind the smuggling operations in Bocka Morrow, damn his eyes if she wasn't.

It was she who had discovered the traitor in their midst, she who had offered Matthew her intimate knowledge of the smuggling operation in order to root out the treason. Without her, Matthew never would have been able to identify the disloyal local curate as the traitor who very nearly succeeded in aiding and abetting Napoleon's planned invasion of their island fortress.

"And how did you find Bocka Morrow, Matthew?" Grace was asking. "I ask because the village is gaining something of a reputation as quite the place to make a match. There have been something like eight or nine betrothals or marriages in the last month alone—our friend Lord Harry Beck included."

Harry's betrothal was no surprise to him—Becks had been well and truly smitten.

But Matthew was still keeping his own guns bowsed up tight behind his port-lids, not giving the game away to Grace, who had both an uncanny intuition and an imagination that traveled in galloping leaps and bounds.

He made his voice everything easy and interested. "Becks is betrothed, is he? To one of the intriguing Teague girls I've no doubt. Nessa, is it?" He also had no doubt as to which one it was—Matthew was quite sure he had personally kept sleepy-eyed Tressa Teague too occupied to intrigue anyone else.

"How do I know that name—Teague?" Owen asked.

"Because of Richard," Grace answered promptly. "It was to the Reverend Teague in Bocka Morrow that Richard went to study theology when he ran away from the navy."

Matthew was stunned into silence—he had not known Richard had lived there, in that town, in that house, with Tressa Teague. Damn, damn, damn his eyes for somehow having missed that information.

"Devil take him, yes!" Owen slapped his plan flat on the table. "Still not sure if I've forgiven him for that—Richard, that is, not this Reverend Teague."

"My darling, if sweet Sally has forgiven Richard, then you must have done with spleen as well," Grace instructed her husband. "But you are diverting me from the salient bit of information in Matthew's speech, which was 'the intriguing Teague *girls*.' More than one, I take it, dear Matthew?"

Damn Grace's perceptive eyes and ears—it was impossible to lie to her.

Matthew settled for as little of the truth as possible. "Oh, aye." He made his voice everything casual.

But Grace was not having it. "I don't recall any mention of local ladies in the report you dictated to me to send to the Admiralty." She gave him a quizzical smile, but her almond-shaped eyes were keen with assessment.

"Aye. Thank you for writing them in your clear and elegant hand—you know my penmanship is rubbish."

"Yes. How interesting." Grace had turned away from reading him like a bloody book, and was reading the calling card Mrs. Jenkins, the housekeeper, brought in. "And, I think, about to get more interesting. For here is our Captain Lord Harry himself to visit us. Show Captain Beck in, Mrs. Jenkins, do."

"Becks!" Matthew rose to greet his friend and former shipmate as if his chest weren't suddenly tight with apprehension. "What brings you to Falmouth?"

"You," Becks was full of cheerful openness. "And a wedding."

"Yours, I hope?" Matthew joked as a stop against his cravat getting any tighter.

"Indeed. Miss Nessa Teague has agreed to make me the happiest man in the world. You may wish me happy."

"I certainly do wish you happy, though I suspected as much." He shook Becks's hand. "And you certainly covered a lot of ground in that cave."

That Matthew had also done some covering of the same ground in that very same cave during a smuggling operation was a topic not to be mentioned—especially in front of Grace, who seemed able to smell a romance the way a terrier scented a rat.

"You'll come, of course, to the wedding to stand up for me?" Harry was asking. "It wouldn't feel right otherwise."

A unfamiliar feeling—something close to panic, judging from the way his heart lurched about in his chest like a sailor on a shore drunk—squeezed up his chest at the thought of having to return to Bocka Morrow. "Are you sure? Surely you have brothers enough to see to the thing?"

Harry winced up one eye. "My brothers are not like yours, Matts—they don't understand. They have no conception of what our lives are like in the navy—how hard it is to be injured and away from service, but also relieved. They can't fathom why I'm near bored to death, but so damned pleased to be so."

"Not bored with your bride I hope?" Matthew steered the conversation from the uncomfortable turn it was taking.

"Bride-to-be—in one week's time. The banns will be read the third and final time by the vicar this Sunday, and we'll marry just as soon as may be after that." When Matthew said nothing, he went on. "Please say you'll come, Kent. I know you're anxious to be off to the West Indies just as soon as your ship is fitted out, but it would mean the world to me if you would consent to come."

"How can you refuse such a pretty invitation?" Grace asked with a smile.

There was nothing for it, of course, except to damn his pride and his promise to stay away from Bocka Morrow and long tall, irresistible Tressa Teague. "When you beg like that, I suppose there is no way for me to refuse. When must I go?"

"Immediately—I'll convey you back to Bocka Morrow myself in my father's traveling coach. It's well sprung and plush, Matts. I intend for us to go out in style."

If he had to go out, Matthew reckoned there was no damn better way to go, than in style. "Lay on, Becks. Lay on."

CHAPTER 4

Village of Bocka Morrow,
Coast of Cornwall
November 23, 1811

OH, HEAVEN HELP HER. He was here—Captain Matthew Kent was standing in the vestry of St. David's, not twelve feet from her.

Tressa's heart slipped and tripped like a maiden aunty drunk on too much elderberry cordial—she had to grip the back of a choir pew to steady herself.

Why had he come?

More to the point, why had no one told her he was coming? How was it possible he was standing with Papa and Lord Harry, looking for all the world as windswept and gallant as if he had just walked off a quarterdeck in his blue naval dress uniform?

She'd known he was a naval officer, of course—she had easily picked out his military bearing even when he had been disguised as a fisherman—but she'd never seen him in anything but knitted wool jumpers and that battered old sea coat he had worn even when commanding his lugger against the French corvette in Black Cove.

But the contrast of the dark blue coat and the flaming red of his ginger hair was so brilliant it near hurt her eyes to look at him. To say nothing of her heart, which was still somehow pumping—still keeping her alive and capable of some small sort of reason—though she had done her best to turn it to stone.

Captain Kent was no doubt acting in support of his brother officer, while Lord Harry's real brothers, Anthony, Viscount Redgrave, and Lord Michael, along with his parents, the Marquess and Marchioness of Halesworth, and his recently married sister Charlotte, now Viscountess Lynwood, sat in the front row across from Mama.

Just as Tressa was attending in support of her sister. She had come to the vestry to announce that Nessa was ready at the door of the church, wearing her pretty bridal ensemble of a dress of fine white wool shot with embroidered primrose and white-satin flowers that she had made and embroidered herself so as not to embarrass herself before Harry's illustrious relations.

But it was Tressa who was now the embarrassment of a bridesmaid, dithering in full view of the assembly. But this was Nessa's day, and Tressa refused to ruin it by her behavior.

"Papa," she called in the steadiest voice she could find. "Nessa is ready." And then she hurried away to attend her sister to the altar and see her bestow her hand upon Lord Harry.

And if Captain Kent stood on the other side of the groom, like a tall oaken mast of a man, she would take no notice of him.

She would not.

It was no matter to her that the gold epaulettes on his uniform coat glistened in the sunlight, or that he and Lord Harry together in their blues looked as dashing as dashing could be. It was no matter than her heart was thumping as if she had raced all the way up to the top of the bell tower of St. David's, and all the way back down again.

It only mattered that she not embarrass her sister, or do anything to dim her happiness.

A surreptitious glance over her shoulder revealed that a good half of the village seemed to have invited themselves, crowding into the pews at the rear of the church, hanging back for propriety's sake, but unable—or unwilling—to turn away from the spectacle of one of the vicar's poor-as-churchmice daughters marrying a lord.

It was every poor village girl's fantasy, she supposed, to marry a man who could sweep her away from gutting fish and scraping scales or cooking on an open fire and cleaning the grates of fireplaces or correcting lessons and writing out sermons.

But her sister Nessa would have loved her Harry if he had only been a sailor. In fact, Tressa would bet both Nessa and Harry would have preferred he be a simple sailor so they could marry with a great deal less pomp and circumstance, even though the wedding was only a simple ceremony in a village church with a wedding breakfast to follow at the vicarage.

But when the "I wills" had been uttered, and the giving and receiving of rings had been exchanged, and the blessing spoken, the crowd of villagers still lingered, following the wedding party across the churchyard and onto the lawn, so that Mama, who could not turn away a chance to show off her daughter, was obliged to invite them all in for a glass of celebratory punch.

In no time, the wedding breakfast had been abandoned in favor of a more informal party that moved easily between the open house and the sunny garden full of autumn color, with avid villagers eager to see the private family rooms of the manse, not just the vicar's book room.

Even Elowen Gannet—she who had once tried to claim Lord Harry for her own—wandered freely about, though her presence gave Tressa's new brother-in-law pause.

"Didn't think to see Miss Gannett here," Harry confided in a low voice.

"Perhaps she wanted to make sure the deed was well and truly done before she moved along to manipulating some other poor fellow into marriage," was Tessa's amused, if cynical take.

"Oh, I think Miss Elowen Gannet has very specific requirement in a husband," Harry said. "Though I am as glad as I can be that chap isn't me—gives me the willies, your Miss Gannett does. She's too bloody ambitious by half—only wanted me to further her scheme to run the smuggling operation in Bocka Morrow without her father's interference."

Tressa pricked up her ears at the same time that Nessa shot her a quelling glance. While it was well-known within the family, and perhaps to some others like Joss Williams, the publican of the Crown & Anchor pub down near the quay, it was generally not known that Tressa was, in fact, the one person who managed the bulk of the smuggling operations—at least on the north side of Bocka Morrow. Tressa had never participated in any free trade to the south, where Squire Gannett kept his own caves and used his own workers.

But as little as Tressa knew or liked the Gannets, perhaps the time for keeping quiet and hiding her ambitions was over. "I think I'll go have a chat with our Ellie."

Who knew if they might find that some of their schemes for less interference were aligned? And Ellie had lost her bid to snag the very-well-worth-having Lord Harry in an Allantide alliance, so Tressa was prepared to be generous.

Tressa waited for Ellie to take her leave, then she snatched up a woolen shawl from the pegs in the kitchen hall as a preservative against the capricious autumn winds and followed her out through the orchard path. "Ellie!"

Her call made her quarry stop and glance back. "Tressa." Ellie acknowledged her with a toss of her chin. "Come to tout your sister's triumph?"

Tressa shrugged. "If it is a triumph, it's hers, not mine."

"Really?" Ellie gave her a long glance out the side of her eye as she tried to gauge Tressa's tone. "Rumor had it that you and that—"

"Rumor is wrong." Tressa spoke perhaps more forcefully that she intended—she lowered her voice to a more conversational pitch. "But I'd like to chat about a different rumor I heard—one that told me that you and I are more alike that we might think."

True to form, Ellie's glance shifted across the churchyard to where Captain Matthew Kent had just stepped outside into the fall sunshine to talk to the Marquess of Halesworth.

"Not a man, Ellie, but something more important." Tressa forced her mind away from the distracting captain and lowered her voice to keep their conversation private. "The management of the free trade."

Ellie's eyes sliced back to Tressa, wary and sharp. "What about it?"

"Surely you know that I organize everything for our crews—unloading, and moving the cargoes on when they come into the north caves?"

"I've heard you keep the tot sheets."

"Yes." It was a sop to the men's pride, that offhand denigration of her true contribution. "And more. I set the crews in the caves. I calculate the price of shares and divvy up the money. I've sailed to Guernsey to arrange financing, pick up cargoes and to better understand the system. I decide what goes where up-country—how many bolts of silk and lace go to Leeds or London, how many ankers of brandy go to this inn or that." Tressa had been the one to suggest the women be included in moving the goods from the caves into cellars across the countryside, and from there to the inns, taverns and aristocratic wine cellars from Truro to Taunton because farmwives could better evade the Revenue with the ankers up their skirts. "I'm the one that has made all the suggestions for improvements over the past few years."

Tressa stopped herself—even she could hear the combination of fierce pride and bitter frustration in her voice. "But that's all I can do, Ellie—make suggestions. I can't decide—not on my own."

Ellie was cautiously curious. "And you think I can?"

"I think you want to." Tressa took another deep breath. "And I think you could. And so could I—with help."

Ellie's voice was quiet. "And you think I would help you?"

"I think we could help each other."

Ellie thought about that suggestion for a good long while, searching Tressa's face for any hint of sarcasm or trick.

"I'm in earnest, Ellie. We could do it. But we'll have to fight for what we want—no one, least of all the men in this be-nighted village, are going to give it to us."

"How will we fight?"

"The way women the world over have always fought—with our wits. We'll be better, more clever, more efficient—we'll make more money."

Ellie's mouth pursed into a silent "o" of shrewd contemplation. "I'm always after telling my Da we could do it better—ordering a cargo of what we want and need in advance from Guernsey instead of taking whatever comes off the boats."

Tressa could feel herself smile. "Just so, Ellie. Just so."

Ellie blew out a little huff of pleased surprise. "Who'd have thought?"

"I did," Tressa admitted. "I've always thought I could do it better."

"No." Ellie shook her head but smiled. "Who would have thought of all the people in Bocka Morrow, the one to want to help me take over the smuggling would be the vicar's daughter. But you always did sit up there in the front row of the church with your family looking like you were a thousand miles away—you and your sister both. Who'd have thought you were thinking of the trade a few miles offshore?"

"I told you—I'm always thinking. Thinking beyond mere smuggling. To a legitimate concern, importing from farther afield—Canary and Sherry wines from Spain."

"And have you thought of how we're to even begin to make that happen?"

"Indeed. We need capital. Once we get enough, we'll run a few smuggled cargoes to build up enough profit to go legitimate, and then—"

Then a quiet voice broke into their conversation.

"Well. Tressa and Ellie Gannett. Whatever can *you* two be talking about?"

CHAPTER 5

*I*T WAS THE BRIDE, Nessa Teague Beck, accompanied by her new husband Harry, who asked the question. Matthew was only with them because Becks had insisted he meet Nessa's sister.

Who shot him a look as mean and cutty-eyed as any smuggler might. "Captain Kent."

"Miss Teague." He bowed, carefully polite, incredibly wary—every instinct he possessed told him Tressa Teague frankly wished him to perdition. "Miss Teague and I are acquainted."

He would do everything in his power to act the gentleman, though she looked like she had even less interest in acting the lady than ever—something he said made her head snap back as if she'd taken a hit.

Beside Becks, his new bride laughed. "Yes, Tressa, you are Miss Teague now. Kensa and I relinquish our turns at the title to you—you are no longer Miss Tressa."

Tressa Teague acknowledged her sister with a nod, and then put her chin up as if she were determined to show that she was not in the least discomfited by the change.

"Captain Kent." She acknowledged him with the barest civility. "Are you acquainted with my friend Miss Gannett? Miss Elowen Gannett, this is Captain Matthew Kent of the Royal Navy frigate, *Vanguard,* which will very shortly be taking command of the West Indies Squadron."

Ah. That boded better—though her tone was brisk, she was still enough interested in him to know the particulars of his posting. "I see news travels fast. I'm honored that you would make note of my promotion."

Tressa Teague gave him a witheringly polite smile. "The announcement was in the newspaper from Truro that we used to wrap the fish."

The knowledge that she was definitely no longer his friend—and the realization that she might, in fact, be his enemy—was a hit to his pride. "May I speak with you privately, Miss Teague?"

While the others—Becks, his bride and Miss Gannett—looked from one to the other, and waited for Tressa to make him her answer, her gaze never wavered. "I am sure that whatever you have to say to me, Captain Kent, can be said in public."

"I am equally sure it cannot." She had tried his civility long enough—he put his hand into the supple small of her back and propelled her away from the others. "The belfry, as I recall, is a private enough place out of the wind." He ushered her across the chilly churchyard and through the portal. "I take it you still have the key?"

"If I do, I shan't be persuaded to— Oooh!" She made a sound of embarrassment and outrage that echoed around the church vestibule like a pistol shot when he abruptly took charge by reaching under the modest fichu of her simple but lovely gown—and what a sweep of bluebell-colored wool it took to cover long, tall Tressa Teague's legs—to fish out the key on the chain hidden down the warm vee of flesh between her breasts.

She was pulled closer, of course, when he fit the key into the lock—so close he could see the care she had taken with her normally indifferent coiffure. So close he could smell that lovely tang of lemon and verbena from her soap.

So close her breath whispered across the back of his hand.

"Here," it whispered. "Here is your woman."

He did not respond. He could not—she didn't *like* him, though she had once kissed him with an enthusiasm he still found heartrending.

Matthew let the key go the moment he had unlocked the door and stood back to let her enter the narrow, stone stairway ahead of him. "After you."

She let the chain back slink back behind the fortress of her high-waisted, devilishly well-fitted bodice before she answered. "You're not planning to push me off, are you?"

"Not if you don't tempt me."

"Clearly, I've worn out your charm." She crossed her hands over her breasts and didn't move. "Why are you here?"

"To celebrate your sister and Harry's wedding. I assure you nothing would have persuaded me to disrupt your peace, otherwise."

"Peace." Her voice was full of cynical detachment. "But I meant here and now—why do you want to speak to me? And drag me up the belfry? What can you possibly have to say that has not already been said?"

Nothing had actually been said. Nothing.

In the aftermath of the battle, he had been consumed by his work—shoring up the damaged French vessel and making arrangement for the hundred or so French sailors they had taken prisoner, as well as formulating his report to the Admiralty—and she had simply disappeared, gone up the quay into the grey mist as swiftly as she had first appeared to him that chilly dawn.

He tried to be his usual bluff, confident self. "I merely wanted to assure myself that you are all to rights—that you had recovered from the ordeal of the battle at Black Cove."

"As you see." She spread her hands in front of her skirts in a gesture that was both open and entirely concealing. "And I didn't think it an ordeal. I told you then, I'm not missish."

"So you did." And she had not looked the least bit missish that night with the wind in her teeth and the tiller of his lugger beneath her hands when he had been too engaged with the heat of battle to notice that she had done what needed doing without being asked.

She had looked magnificent.

"You had a heart of oak that night. I suppose I wanted to make sure it was still beating in tune."

She swallowed some rising emotion before she said, "Not to your tune, if that is what you meant."

"No. I—" Damn her eyes, but she had a way of looking at him—as if she saw right through him—that put a man off balance.

He knew what to do with a ship—how to order his sails and level his guns against an enemy—but in a drawing room, or even in a bell tower, he felt himself an utter ass.

"Come, Teague, I know I left very suddenly, but orders are orders, and—"

"It's Miss Teague to you, Captain Kent."

Her prim—yes, missish tone, when she had just said she wasn't—pushed him a fathom too far. "It wasn't Miss Teague, or Captain Kent, when you were kissing me, was it?"

The moment the words left his mouth he wished them back. But that was his problem, wasn't it—acting on the impulse of the moment, instead of weighing things out.

She drew in a sharp breath before she put her chin up

even higher. "Were I closer to you, Captain, I would have slapped you. Hard." Her voice was taut with repressed emotion. "Just because we kissed does not mean you can speak to me in such a manner. Now"—she backed away as if to preserve herself from the temptation, rubbing her hands up and down her arms as if she were suddenly chilled—"say what you brought me here to say, and be done with it before I find myself in any less charity to listen to you."

Matthew had already stripped off his uniform coat and was advancing to sling it around her shoulders before he had even thought to ask her if she should like it. But she was a difficult, prickly girl—everyone said so—and was like to catch her death of a chill before she would ask for any assistance.

But for some reason, she didn't reject the coat. "Well? You interrupted a very important discussion that I should like to return to, if Ellie hasn't already given up and gone home."

"Aye. And just what was it you and the devious Miss Gannett were cooking up?"

He had distinctly heard Nessa mutter, 'This can't be good,' before she had dragged her husband and Matthew out into the churchyard.

"My business with Miss Gannett is no business of yours. Though, how typical of a man to use 'cooking up'—the language of the kitchen or the coven—to describe any instance of two women working together."

"Working together?" Matthew couldn't keep the astonishment, or the instinctive alarm, from his voice. "In the smuggling?"

The sheer bloody cheek of this woman, presuming to tell a captain of the navy—and the very man who had been sent to their bloody village to put the fear of God, or at least the fear of His Majesty's Royal Navy, into the smuggling gangs—

that she was planning to ally with another smuggler, to not only continue, but perhaps even expand—

His bloody brain boggled.

And she knew it—she gave him a smile of pure cussed determination. "You understand me, Captain. We *do* intend to use our womanly wiles to take over the whole of the free trade on this cursed, backward coast, and make it our own."

CHAPTER 6

THE LOOK ON HIS FACE—the gaping combination of anger and alarm—was entirely worth the trouble of being frog-marched across the churchyard. Let him think she had no scruples—that her plans were for the smuggling and not legitimate trade.

Because he had inadvertently, through his ham-fisted questions, given her the answer to her own question—where was she to get the capital for her own company to compete against the free trade?

From the kitchen and the coven—from Bocka Morrow's women.

She would build her own syndicate, the way they did at Lloyd's Society in London. Selling shares only to women could, of course, be problematic. So few women had control of their own finances—only widows or heiresses with significant allowances would have the freedom to invest large sums of money on their own account.

But Bocka Morrow had a significant—some might even say shocking—number of women quite willing and determined to make their own way in the world and command their own fate. Tressa would safely bet that she could sell as many small shares in a syndicate as she might like.

But as to larger shares—firstly, there was her sister, now Lady Harry Beck, who would have an allowance with which she might be persuaded at least in part, to contribute. And her sister might be able to quietly persuade some of her new acquaintances, like her new sister-in-law, Charlotte, Viscountess Lynwood over at Hollybrook Park, and Charlotte's husband's sisters, the Ladies Diana, Miranda, Cordelia and Adriana Vail. Or the Earl of Banfield's five daughters, Ladies Tamsyn, Marjorie, Rose, Morgan, and Gwyn Hambly —a wonderful assortment of the female portion of the local upper crust ripe for convincing that their allowances might be put to profitable use.

And the other person besides her sister who might help her with some entrée into aristocratic society was Tressa's dear friend, confidant and oftentimes confederate, Felicity Fields, the ward of the late Countess of Tetbery. While Felicity didn't always understand the subtle ins and outs of society, she was sure to understand Tressa's bid for more independence, since she often bemoaned her own lack thereof. But with the countess dead, and the estate passing to some far-off male relative, Felicity was clearly better advised to save her pennies to put a secure roof over her head.

Still, Tressa could ask. And there were others in more aristocratic circles Tressa knew only through Felicity—women who moved between both worlds, town and castle—like Lady Mallory Hughes.

Yes, a secret syndicate of women was entirely doable, now that she put her mind to it.

But before she could consult with Felicity, Tressa needed to be rid of the interfering, too-brazenly-handsome-for-anyone's-good captain.

"If you're done playing the stern naval captain, then I'll

get on playing the devious lady smuggler. I bid you good afternoon, Captain Kent."

Tressa tossed him his coat so his hands would be too busy catching it to stop her from whisking herself out of the tower and around to the back of the church through the shrubbery.

But without Kent's coat to keep off the chill, Tressa was best advised to keep to a brisk pace to stay warm. The long shadows of the November afternoon reached chilly fingers through the woods as she hurried through Bent Tree Copse and along the edge of Hollybrook land to reach Tetbery, silently rehearsing the right words to explain her idea to her friend.

She didn't bother with the main entrance of the gothic pile, with its bedraggled black crepe and knocker still down following the countess's death some five months ago. Instead, she skirted the grey stone castle until she found the path leading down into the now-dry moat, overgrown with brambles and briars and ivy that kept the less tenacious from accessing a long abandoned postern door set low in the old curtain wall. From there she followed the curving set of secret stairs upwards through the walls, without disturbing anyone in the house.

Felicity was just where Tressa had hoped to find her— attired in another one of the inky black, practical dresses she'd worn since the death of her guardian last summer, in her quiet work room, hidden from all but the most determined gaze in one of Tetbury's secret chambers, bent over some experiment. Which thankfully did not look to be a-boil.

"I've got a proposition for you, Fieldsy," Tressa said by way of greeting, for social niceties were lost on Felicity, who looked as fey and wild as a red fox in a field but had a brain that worked as flawlessly as a mechanical clockwork—albeit a clockwork with its own unique timing.

Her friend's answering frown was nearly imperceptible to anyone who didn't know Felicity well. "Does it involve going out of the house?"

"No." Tressa never minded her friend's rather blunt style of talking. In fact, she rather preferred such straightforwardness to the broth of double-speak, platitudes and outright lies most people served up as conversation. And she liked being straightforward herself. "I've decided to run my own shipping firm."

Felicity's green eyes barely flicked toward her, but Tressa knew her friend had likely taken in more information in that fleeting gaze than most people could absorb in a month of staring directly at her. "That's logical—you want power over the men."

"No. Not really. Perhaps." There was no use dancing around the issue with Felicity. "I only want power over myself, and my own life, but to do so it seems I must first take it from the men. And to do that I need money. Have you got any?" While Tressa knew Felicity had no fortune from her own family—her deceased parents had been quality, but not particularly rich when they had died years ago, leaving her the ward of the Earl and Countess of Tetbery—Tressa hoped her friend might have inherited something of her own when Margaret, the countess, had passed away.

"The countess did leave me a small bequest." Felicity looked away from her notebook for only a moment. "What is the money for?"

"Shares in a syndicate—a syndicate *only* of women. I'm fed up to the back teeth with doing all the work and getting none of the credit—and even less of the profit than the men."

"Men," was Felicity's terse response. "It's always the men."

"Yes." Tressa had not forgotten the particular limbo in which Felicity currently hung after five months of waiting for the bane of their youth, Nicholas Harding, the Duke of

Wycliffe, and the lord of Tetbury Estate, to come and take up his place. And decide what was to be done with Felicity—as if Fieldsy couldn't possibly decide that for herself. "Have you heard anything more?"

"No. Nicholas has not written of his plans for Tetbury. Or me."

"Oh, I am sorry, Fieldsy."

"Why?" Felicity meticulously cleaned her pen before she put it down. "It's not your doing."

"No." Tressa had long ago given up trying to explain social niceties to Felicity. "Were it in my power, I should have made Nicholas act in a civil and logical manner to you, and make his plans known to you directly he inherited this moldy old pile. But lords of the manor can do as they please, it seems." They could treat all women with indifference to their merit or needs. "I'll have my father write him to remind him of his duty."

In actuality, Tressa would write the letter and simply sign her father's name—it was the most expedient way of getting things done. Always had been.

"I wish you wouldn't. I prefer him forgetting Tetbury and me altogether. I like this moldy old pile—it's my home. He's sure to put an end to my work when he comes."

Tressa took a moment to canvass the room and the delicate scaffolding erected on the table to support the vials and flasks of Felicity's current experiment. "What are you working on now?" Over the years of their friendship, Felicity had studied everything from plant biology to animal husbandry.

"Still the alchemy."

"Ah." Not the answer Tressa had been hoping for. While her friend was forever picking up one specimen or another in the woods, or down at the seashore, and studying them to exhaustion, she seemed to have developed an unhealthy mania for the study of alchemy, with the sole purpose of discovering the elixir of life.

Though Tressa believed in scientific study as much—and even more—than the next person, she would not materially support a study that seemed sure to break Felicity's heart. "I wish I could dissuade you from this path."

Felicity was characteristically determined. "I must exhaust all possibilities through study."

Strange, but still logical. And Tressa needed to be logical, too—she couldn't take Felicity's money, not when the poor girl might soon have need of it to put a roof over her head. But there were others in Felicity's small orbit who might have more ready capital.

"Does Lady Mallory have any money do you think?" Lady Mallory Hughes would soon be visiting Tetbury with her ancient, but delightfully formidable aunt, Lady Hettie Hughes. And while both the young lady and her aunt were merely acquainted with Tressa, she was determined to let no female stone go unturned. "Or Lady Hettie?"

"I have never discussed funds with Mallory. Nor you. Do you have none?"

"I have some—the meager portion of my pay for the cargoes that I've been allowed to keep."

That she had *earned* far more than she was given was another reason to strike out on her own—the powers that be in the free trading confraternity still paid her father, even though they clearly knew and relied upon her to do the work.

"Is Nessa married then?"

While the question didn't startle Tressa, it was uncharacteristic of Felicity to want to chat about such thing. "Yes, to Captain Lord Harry. I'm sure they'll be very happy."

Felicity sighed. "Someone ought to be."

"*We* ought to be," Tressa assured her. "Even if it's not

marriage that makes us happy." Tressa couldn't stop her impulse to touch Felicity's hand in friendship before she took her leave. "Send me a note, will you, when Lady Mallory and her aunt arrive?"

Even small amounts would be helpful, as she could then go to the bankers in Saint Peter Port in Guernsey—who routinely made loans to finance free-traded cargoes—with assets in hand as a surety.

Yes, that was likely her best, most logical avenue of approach—the ladies of Bocka Morrow first, the bankers of Guernsey second. And after that, the wide open world could be her oyster.

With that expansive thought in mind, Tressa took the long coastal path home to ponder out whom else she might approach. But backward as it was, the beauty of Bocka Morrow filled her mind and her weary heart. The green grass of the cliff tops had already begun its slow fade into autumn gold, the heaps of flowering thrift giving way to the dark brooding gorse, especially on the wild fringes of Castle Keyvnor land, where the Widow Pencomb's cottage clung like a limpet to the cliff top.

The widow herself was at the door of her cottage, as if in her eerie way, she had been expecting Tressa—it was no wonder the better part of the population of Bocka Morrow thought the old woman a witch.

But Tressa was not of the better part. She looked the old woman in the eye and knew her for a rebellious, kindred spirit. "Good afternoon, mistress."

"Tressa Teague. My gratulations to your sister on her wedding. I reckon you've come to ask me for more of the same that I gave her to enchant her young man."

Even though Tressa had encouraged her sister to visit the widow in search of an enchantment, Tressa was not of the same mind. "I have not. I've no truck with enchantment."

"Haha! You're not like your sister, are ye? Always questioning, wondering is Nessa. But not ye. Ye've an answer to every question, and a question for every answer."

"To my thinking, the world could use a few more women who know their own mind. Like you."

"Ah, but I'm special." The old woman gave her a creaky, wry smile. "I know me own worth, as ye sometimes appear to. But I'm no vicar's daughter, Tressa Teague. Ye've to answer to a different power than I."

"I'll answer to my own power, and none other, thank you."

"Haha!" The old woman tossed her head back to loose another harsh laugh. "You're a rare girl, Tressa Teague, I'll say that for ye. And I'm thinking he's a rare enough man to appreciate ye, that captain of yourn."

Tressa felt her neck flush with mortification that anyone might know her business—even a busybody old witch. "He's not my captain."

"Is he not? Whose else is he, if not yourn?" The widow let out a raucous cackle. "Open yer eyes, girl. Open them up wide enough to see how that man looks at ye—as if ye were the last spoonful of water on the flat earth and he, dying for a drop."

"Good heavens." Tressa was beyond astonished—she was decidedly curious. "Does he really?" She couldn't imagine such a man doing any such thing.

"He does look at ye different—as if ye were a rare and beautiful thing. And that is a thing very much worth having in this world, Tressa Teague. Ye might not find it's like again."

Tressa knew she would not. Because she had given up looking. "He is leaving—bound for the West Indies. I should expect he's already gone."

"And ye let him go?"

What else was she to do? "I'll not chase after him like some silly, moonstruck calf."

"You're no calf, and you're no lamb to the slaughter, neither. But were I ye, I'd not waste me chance. I'd go to him and hash it out betwixt the two of ye, and no one else. For how else are ye to come to a right agreement."

"A right agreement?" It had never really occurred to Tressa that a woman could have a real, true agreement—especially an agreement of the heart—with a man.

"Nothing more," the old woman assured her. "And nothing less."

CHAPTER 7

MATTHEW HAD TRIED to follow Tressa, but she'd made it damn near impossible with her blazingly swift, surefooted passage through the woods. He was a navy man, at home in the vast expanse of the sea—the closed sky of the dense woodland made him uneasy. Uneasy enough to return to the church and avail himself of the still-unlocked door to the tall, airy belfry, from whence he could keep an eye on the whole of the village, just as she had taught him.

And it would do him no good to try and chase a lass like Tressa Teague—she'd have to come to him of her own accord.

The sun was beginning to set, burnt orange and cool purple over the cold ocean stretching endlessly to the west, when she did so, striding down the narrow, cobbled streets as if she owned them. No decorous miss, Tressa Teague.

There was something about her, something knowing and wise and too-old for the young, lissome form that had her standing as tall, if not taller, than most of the men in the village.

She was also blonder than any Cornishwoman had a right to be—like something from the Norse myths—an avenging Valkyrie from the north. Except for those sleepy, knowing eyes. She looked as if nothing would surprise her—as if she'd seen it all before.

And clearly, she had seen him coming.

"Teague!"

She stopped when he called down to her and was waiting when he descended to the church door. "I thought you would be off to the West Indies by now."

He cleared his throat and made his voice stern and forbidding, the better to lie more convincingly. "Some further orders require that I stay here to clear up the last of this business."

"Just now?" She narrowed her eyes in suspicion. "While you were at the wedding, the Admiralty chased you down at the top of the belfry to give you further orders?"

Damn her sharp eyes—it was damn near eerie how she could make his collar feel too tight.

"What did you do this time to incur the Admiralty's wrath?"

The notch in his collar strangled itself tighter. Her acuity was a like a sharp pebble in his sea boots—uncomfortable at best, and damn near crippling at worst. "I should worry about myself, were I you—you're the one talking about expanding the smuggling, when after this last incident, you ought to be doing everything in your power to control and even curtail it, given what's happened."

"What happened, Captain Kent, was that I helped you catch a traitor," she said clearly. And just as clearly, she was done with helping now.

Matthew tried another tack. "If you won't think of yourself, think of your family. Think of Nessa and Harry—think how it would be for a sister of a Royal Navy captain to be taken up for smuggling."

"Taken up for what? Chatting into my punch cup at a wedding? Do be sure to take my father, the vicar, up as well, while you're at it—and the magistrate, and Squire Gannett, not to mention the Earl of Banfield, the Marquess of Halesworth, and the Viscount Lynwood. They've been at the smuggling, and the punch, far longer than I."

"You know damn well what I mean, Teague. I see the sharp look in your otherwise sleepy eyes, and I know you're up to no good."

"It's a very short memory you have, Captain, to be forgetting that you never would have caught your traitor without me, and without the villagers—the poor fisherfolk and farmers who came to your aid that night and sacrificed nigh unto a six-month's worth of French brandy and Holland gin and Belgian lace that went up in flames in Black Cave along with your munitions, with nary a cry for relief." She put up her chin and stepped closer to deliver her last salvo. "And *you* know damn well that I never would have helped you if I hadn't been convinced that the powers that be—from the magistrates to the Revenue Service and up to the Admiralty—would leave us in peace as payment for our sacrifice."

Devil take her, but she was right.

Still. "Thanking you for your past assistance doesn't give you immunity from future prosecution."

"It ought to do—the Admiralty ought to have a better strategy than to send you back to bite the hand that fed you."

"The Admiralty's strategies are none of your business."

"Just as my strategies for how to make my way in this world are none of yours," she shot back. "It's no fault of mine that my strategies are simply better than the Admiralty's. Or yours—I would have interrogated those hundred French prisoners from that corvette that night far more closely had I been in command, to find out what they knew of Gravelines, from whence they sailed. You do know about Gravelines, do you not, Captain? How Napoleon built his open secret of an entrepôt on the north coast of France to encourage British smugglers to betray their country simply by their easy trade with the enemy—to help the British free traders evade tax is to keep revenue from the Admiralty's coffers, is it not? I should have taken a man or two of those French sailors apart for a friendly chat before I stuffed them all below decks and hied off to Portsmouth."

Oh, damn, damn, damn her brilliant brain. "How do you know I didn't do exactly that while underway to Portsmouth?"

"Because I was there. And because you're here, harrying me, instead of sailing up the canal at Gravelines and setting fire to those warehouses, the way your sister—who by all accounts sounds like twice the sailor of at least half of her brothers—did when she set flame to the whole port of Brest in the year five."

Matthew ground his teeth together to keep from gaping at her like a fish gasping for water upon dry land. "How do you know about that?" His younger sister Sally's misadventure six years ago as a midshipman in the Royal Navy remained a closely guarded family secret. "And it wasn't like that—she didn't single-handedly sail in there—"

"No, she had a vastly superior strategy of her own—a strategy that she proved successful."

"How do you know that?" he asked again.

"Come, Captain. You came here as a spy—surely you knew your brother Richard lived here, with us. And while he did, he told my father all. He—Richard, not my father—might have been shocked and mortified by your sister's actions, but I was delighted. And enthralled."

"You would be, you bloody pirate."

"Thank you." She took his grousing as a compliment. Which it probably was—unlike Richard, Matthew had admired Sally's guts in going aboard ship in Richard's place. "And I pledged as a girl to let her be my example for how to get what I wanted in this life, no matter the obstacles or objections."

Matthew didn't like being one of those obstacles, but he had no choice but to object—not to do so would put her in jeopardy, from which he might not be able to extract her. "You make it sound as if she were the captain of her own ship, and I assure you she was not. And she was with her husband, under whose guidance—"

"Captain Colyear wasn't her husband at the time, nor even her captain."

"The point is, she's married now—"

"To Captain Colyear, and sails with him, aboard his ship, *Audacious*."

"*His* ship, I hope you'll note."

"Oh, yes, so noted. And I'm *sure* she sits still and waiting all day in his stern cabin, just knitting or gazing idly out the windows, and *never* lifts so much as a finger to help her husband. And he *never* consults with her. I am sure they are both quite happy to let that superior brain of hers—all that acumen and experience and *strategy*—go to waste. I'm quite sure."

Devil take her. "*How* do you know all this?"

Her smile was triumphant. "I wrote her, those six years ago, when Richard complained so bitterly about her, for I thought she was a woman I should like to know. So I imposed upon the very slight connection and wrote, and your sister wrote me back. We still correspond to this day—whenever she happens upon a ship bound to England, or finds herself in port, she writes me. I've learned a marvelously shocking amount of the world from your sister."

"Devil take Sal for encouraging susceptible females."

"Susceptible? Is that what you think I am? I assure you, I am not in the least bit susceptible or manageable."

"You were definitely susceptible to me, and to my kisses."

"My dear Captain Kent." Her tone was nearly pitying. "Did you think you were romancing my co-operation out of me?" She tipped her head over and smiled in that damned sleepy, come-hither-but-do-so-and-I-will-box-your-ears way of hers. "Did it never occur to you that I might be the one seducing you into ridding me of that meddlesome priest?"

"The devil you were." And to prove it, he kissed her.

CHAPTER 8

*T*HIS KISS WAS NOTHING like the mischievous charm of the very first time his smiling lips had touched hers a month ago. One month—he had been gone from her only one month, but with his mouth pressed to hers, it felt as if it might have been a year, or ten, or twenty the way he kissed her simply, forcefully, with all the want and curiosity and conflict that had wound up between them like a cargo of dangerous, incendiary black powder.

And heaven help her if she didn't want to strike the match to set them alight.

Tressa's hand flexed and gripped his shoulders, holding on as tight as she dared. She had waited so long for someone who seemed to want her exactly as she was—without wanting *less* from her. Who goaded her into *more*.

Lord knew she found him easy—easy to kiss, if not easy to trust. Everything about him shouted charm and capability and confidence. He set his mouth flush against her lips, and let his breath mix and mingle with hers, while his hands stole along the line of her jaw, angling her head to his liking.

And oh, how she liked. She tipped her head away, offering

him greater access to the sensitive skin along the side of her neck. Offering him her own confidence. Offering him her own passionate curiosity.

She was certainly a curious girl—always had been. And she had always been curious about kissing—enough to try it a time or two with one boy or another. But nothing in those sloppy, awkward kisses had prepared her for *him*.

For the taste of him, of mint and brandy and excitement. For the smell of him, of soap and clean linen beneath the dark wool uniform coat. For the feel of his hands around her head and along the line of her jaw, urging her to kiss him more, to kiss him deeper. For the strength of his long, lean leg where his thigh snugged up next to hers.

For the power that she was so willing to cede to him—at least for a little while.

It was heaven. It was bliss. Bliss lighting up her lips and skin and breath, until she couldn't breathe and didn't need to, because all she wanted was him.

Bliss that made every taste and touch a hundred times stronger, a thousand times more powerful. Bliss that made her want to curl up inside it and abide there, just for a little while, where there was no navy or smugglers, no trouble or strife, or need for syndicates.

Where there was only the two of them giving each other such unrestrained pleasure.

"Devil take me," he mouthed into her ear. "But I want you, Teague."

"I want you, too, Kent." A needy sort of greed was welling up within her. Her hand tightened, flexing into the lapel of his coat, pulling him closer, holding him near.

He reached up and enmeshed his fingers with hers, pressing their hands together between them, and the strange, careful intimacy of the gesture undid something wary and watchful within her.

"Matthew," she said, because she couldn't think, and because it seemed the right thing to say. And when his name fell from her lips, his eyes crinkled and his mouth came open on a wide, welcoming smile—a gift she meant to take.

The feel of his firm lips beneath hers was extraordinary, and she was conscious of listening to him—to his breathing and low murmurs of encouragement. Of trying to go slowly, to savor every touch, every taste.

And so was he. "Handsomely now, Tressa Teague."

She could not comprehend him. "What does that mean?"

"It's a navy term," he murmured into her ear. "Meaning with all due deliberation and attention to detail."

She very much liked his details—his lips were chapped and rough from years at sea, but the moment he opened his mouth to her, she fell into the inexpressible intoxication of him. He kissed with a mischievous, roguish glee—as if he could think of nothing better—and with a sureness that left her breathless and racing to catch up. But when she would have taken his face between her hands and turned her head to follow the dark, twisty path of her desires, he drew back.

"Don't look at me like that."

"Like what?" Like a calf-eyed girl, idiot enough to kiss a man on the steps of her father's church?

"As if I've just offered you the moon. I haven't. It was just a kiss, lass."

As if her wanting to kiss him meant she was offering anything more. She was guarding her heart if not her virtue. Still. "It was a bloody good kiss."

He couldn't master his smile—it spread across his face like the moonlight dancing upon the water. "Thank you. But it is also a kiss that is over."

"Why?" Why should she not take what she wanted when she wanted?

"Because if I don't stop kissing you, Teague, I shall start

doing other things. And it is cold, and falling dark, and we are in front of your father's church in the middle of the village and someone is bound to see us."

His speech was entirely logical. But perhaps she wanted to be something less than logical and reasoned at the moment. "Maybe I want the other things, Kent."

He smiled, that mischievous, merry smile that creased up the corners of his glittering eyes and made a slash of white of his teeth. "If you aren't the damnedest girl for a vicar's daughter."

"Am I? Well, I suppose I am. I like to choose for myself. And I won't be sorry for choosing you and kissing you—it was bloody marvelous."

He laughed and shook his head. "Devil take me, Tressa Teague."

"No." She made up her mind. "I don't think I'm going to let the devil have you. I rather want you for my own."

Oh, he liked that, Matthew Kent did—he threw his head back and laughed out loud. "I keep forgetting how frank you are."

"I told you—I'm not missish. I have educated myself to be a rational creature, with dominion over my emotions. Like you."

"My dear Teague"—he shook his head in teasing sadness—"if you think I have dominion over my emotions, you overestimate me," he laughed. "I am as susceptible to the impulse of the moment as anyone I know. Probably more so, because I want to give in to my impulse to kiss you again."

"I wish you would." And to encourage him, she slid closer, and looped her arm about his neck.

But he did not yet kiss her. Instead he took her jaw in his hands, fanning his palms across her cheeks, as if he might try to read her in the wash of light from the moon. "You're all gilded in moonlight. But for all your gloss and glitter, I still can't make you out, Tressa Teague."

There was something solemn, and even a little frightening in the focus of his regard. As if he might in the next moment find what he was looking for in her face and find her wanting. Or difficult.

"I am as you see," she whispered, not knowing what more she could do to gain his confidence. No matter his frown, when he looked at her like that, she longed for him to kiss her again. She wanted to feel the little shivers that ran tingling along her spine when he had run his hands up her arms and sent the delicious curling heat deep down inside her.

In those moments, Tressa was completely and excruciatingly aware of Matthew Kent as a man, a vibrant, physical being—and a man she wanted. His presence was like a pressure—like the energy in the air when a storm was about to sweep up from the sea and batter the village.

The scientific books she had read up in the belfry would have called it dynamics and set forth an equation to illustrate mutual force and reciprocal attraction. But an equation could not explain why her fingers itched to feel the short strands of his ginger hair, or why her lips longed for the strong feel of his mouth on hers, or why the ache that seemed to have become a part of her dissolved into nothingness the moment he pulled her into his arms.

He kissed her and nothing else existed. Nothing but heat and texture and scent. The supple warmth of his mouth on hers, the raspy feel of his skin against her cheek, the tangy soapy aroma of his body.

He pulled her flush against the long strength of his body, his hand spanning the small of her back, and she flowed into him, pliant and wanting, fitting herself into every breath of space between them. His other hand was at her nape, cradling her skull, angling her head to take her mouth, to fill her with the caress of his tongue upon hers.

Warmth spread from her belly throughout her body, and she was floating, swimming in sensation, plunging in headfirst, immersing herself in the dark liquid depths of desire.

She pulled back to stare at him as he had stared at her—framing his face with her hands, committing the map of his to her memory. She could look at him for days and still not be done looking. The broad plan of his forehead, the strong cut of his cheekbones, the firm line of his jaw. The darkened, silvered blue of his eyes, and the two lines of laughter that were permanently etched into their corners.

She put her lips to his, to let the pleasure sweep her under and carry her away on the tide. Away from worry and duty. Away from the free trade and traitors, and toward Matthew.

Matthew, who kissed her as if she were vital to his happiness, as if he would breathe her in instead of the cold autumn air. As if he did not want to let her go.

CHAPTER 9

HE HAD TO LET HER GO—or suffer the consequences. For all her talk of wanting other things, she was still the daughter of the village vicar, and they were still kissing on the doorstep of the church—if he were a more religious man, he might have feared the proverbial bolt of lightning.

But he'd already been struck, hadn't he—by the *coup de foudre*. That was why he was still kissing Tressa Teague on the very doorstep of her father's church.

And if he were being entirely honest with himself, she had hit him with another bolt. The idea she had so briefly outlined—the setting of a fireship into Napoleon's den of smugglers at Gravelines—had already taken up residence in the back of his brain.

He was already casting his mind back, to the night in Black Cove—the dark outline of the French corvette silhouetted against the grey, looming cliffs, and then the hot flash and thunder of the explosion and the orange blossom of the fire. Remembering Tressa Teague—the one person in Bocka Morrow who had trusted him enough to work relentlessly with him to root out the traitor—taking up the abandoned helm of the lugger in the heat of battle, not shirking away from any danger, not flinching from any duty, no matter how perilous.

It was coming back to him—the images vivid in his mind of that night. He could picture her now, speaking to the French captain in his own language—her father was a schoolmaster, and she was annoyingly well-read—and passing Matthew's orders to the captured prisoners.

"What did they tell you, the French prisoners?"

She drew back slowly, those gloriously sleepy eyes blinking at him in confusion for the barest moment before they lit in amusement. "You can't resist, can you? Impulsive Matthew Kent—you're already halfway there in your mind, aren't you, sailing for the French coast by the feel of the waves without so much as a chart, or a by-your-leave from the Admiralty?"

Devil take him, but she was right—he could all but feel the deck beneath his feet. The possibility was intoxicating. And what were his family's watchwords? "'If you are successful no questions will be asked,'" he quoted. "'And if you fail no explanation will ever be enough.'"

Her expression sobered. "Kent, isn't that how you got yourself in trouble—dis-rated and stripped of your command? Isn't that why you were sent to Bocka Morrow in the first place?"

"That was different." He had learned from his mistakes—and he would be sure not to fail. "I didn't have you to help me the way I did at Black Cove." Matthew could feel his excitement rise like a tide within him, filling him with confidence. "I didn't have your stratagems and plans and more prudent reasoning. I didn't have you to give me the devil's own luck."

The smile lingering in the corner of her eyes warmed a

degree or two in the crisp fall air, as if perhaps his enthusiasm were beginning to infect her reason. "We were lucky that night in Black Cove—lucky there wasn't an invasion fleet at our backs. We'd all be speaking French in Bocka Morrow had they come upon us so unprepared."

"So, we will be prepared for Gravelines. You can help me prepare." If there were other reasons to ask for her assistance—reasons that had more to do with her unreasonably confident kisses than her reasonable brain—he would keep them to himself. "Come with me," he cajoled. "Show me how it can be done."

He gave her the merry, mischievous smile that had always smoothed his way through life.

"You know you want to," he pressed. "I am offering you just the kind of opportunity—the kind of adventure—you've been waiting for and wanting your whole life. We'll be partners—with equal shares in the endeavor."

She drew in a deep breath, but though there was a small smile brewing on her lips, she still regarded him critically. "Equal. I understand what your reward will be—if my plan works, you shall be famous and feted and no doubt given a medal or two."

"Perhaps." He was not undertaking such a fraught undertaking for any reward from the Admiralty, but for a more personal reason—her.

"But *I* shall not be rewarded," she pressed. "I was not rewarded last time, with a share of the French corvette, though you would not have captured it without my information and assistance."

"Damn if you aren't right, Teague." Normally a prize of the French corvette's size would be divided up between ninety-odd men, but Matthew had only had a handpicked crew of sixteen in Bocka Morrow. With a captain and two mates, the remaining fourteen men would earn more money in one night than they had in years of regular pay once the prize was adjudicated. And there was 'head money' for each of the hundred or so French prisoners on top of that. With such a prize, he would finally have the independent fortune he had been working toward throughout the entirety of his career.

"It's because I'm a woman, though you said to me that night that I had a heart of oak, that none of your lieutenants could have done better."

"I did." He had actually forgotten her in the heat of battle and was more than amazed that she had kept so cool a head—he had been impressed. "And I meant it—you were spectacular. And to prove it, I will pay you a full half of my share of that French corvette."

He was rewarded for his impulsive generosity by her expression—her mouth, that perfect, wide, kissable mouth, opened in a silent 'o' of utter astonishment. "If you come with me," he coaxed, "we'll be pirates together, you and I, outside of the rule of the Admiralty. Equal partners.

Those usually sleepy eyes were shining with excitement. "Give me your hand."

There was no question but that he would agree—he would have agreed at twice the price. Because without her, he could not hope to succeed. He stuck out his hand. "Agreed. You have my word."

"As an officer of His Majesty's Navy and a gentleman, or as a pirate?"

"Both, for they are one and the same."

"Agreed. Thank you." She let go of his hand before he could make good on the impulse to pull her tight and kiss his on the lips to seal their bargain.

The excitement dimmed from her face when she looked across the churchyard toward the vicarage. "When do we leave?"

"Just as soon as I can commandeer a ship." There was at least some part of the planning that he was competent enough to see to. "Is the lugger still tied up at the quay where we left it?"

She narrowed her eyes and corrected him. "Where *I* left it? Aye."

He had originally forgotten the fishing boat—in the immediate aftermath of the battle in Black Cove, he had taken control of the larger corvette, setting his crew to repair enough of the damage his guns had carved into the hull to keep her afloat and make her seaworthy enough to sail into Portsmouth for adjudication. Teague had seen to the lugger. "Are the guns still on her?"

She gave him an arch look. "Did you not notice when you were up in my tower, trying to keep track of me?"

He had not, damn his eyes. He had only looked for the girl.

She shook her head at him. "Details, Kent. Details. The guns were there last morning. But I had plans for that lugger."

"Change them—you're too good to be a mere smuggler, Teague."

The look on her face was the most beautiful combination of astonishment and calm understanding. "I know."

"Excellent." He could feel his grin spread wide across his face—he hadn't felt this happy, this damn excited, in months. "I'll go now and have a look at her and see if anything needs to be put aright." He looked across the churchyard toward the quiet vicarage, its warm windows spilling welcoming light into the night. "I'll come back, in the morning, shall I? To see if you're still game."

To give her the night to make sure. To see if cooler heads would prevail.

"No," she said quietly, seemingly determined to be as rashly impetuous as he. "I'll come to you."

"All right." Something within him had him reaching to brush a loose wisp of her fine golden hair off her cheek. And then he leaned in, to kiss her on the forehead. And then once more on her berry-soft lips.

So she would know—she would know without a doubt, what she would be saying yes to. "Be sure of yourself, Teague. Or don't come at all."

CHAPTER 10

TRESSA PASSED a long, sleepless night. The room she had until then always shared with her sister felt empty. Nessa had packed away all her things—every last piece of clothing and linen—into her trunks in preparation for her new life with Lord Harry. One of the trunks still stood by the door, awaiting a final direction once Nessa and Harry were returned from their honeymoon trip and had decided upon a more permanent abode.

If the choice had been Tressa's, she would have wanted to go with Lord Harry upon his ship. She would have chosen to see the world.

But so she already had—the only difference was the man with whom she would see at least a portion of it. Captain Matthew Kent was as different a man from Lord Harry as chalk was from cheese. Matthew Kent was ambitious, and his ambitions would always come before all else.

Before family. Maybe even before country. And certainly before her.

In the past that driving ambition had suited her—it worked to her advantage to have his ruthless determination in removing the traitor from their midst. But in the aftermath of the battle, Kent had instantly forgotten about her very existence—he had climbed aboard the French prize ship and never looked back.

And so he would again, once she had helped him with the scheme she had so foolishly suggested to him.

But help him she would, for there was no other way for her to gain her rightful share of the prize money for the French ship.

And if she did not leave Bocka Morrow—where nothing was new, and nothing would ever change—she might never again have the chance. If she stayed her life would be the same—days would turn into seasons, and seasons would turn into years, and years would turn into centuries while everything stayed the same but the aging faces of the people.

And so, it was she who had to change. To take a chance when it was offered, no matter how imperfect a chance it might be.

Tressa rose from her bed in the dark grey light before dawn. She donned her warmest, sturdiest, plainest wool gown, and took up her heavy winter cloak and the small cloth bag into which she had put a few personal necessities. She smoothed back the covers on the bed, laid the two careful notes she had penned upon it—one to her parents, and one to dear Felicity, who was likely to worry more than Tressa's parents if Tressa simply disappeared—and crept silently down the back stairs, taking care to step over the third to last stair that creaked so horribly.

"Tressa?" Her father's voice, thin and quiet. "Is that you?"

She didn't allow herself the luxury of hesitation. "No." Her whisper was all for herself as she eased the garden door closed behind her. Because she was not his daughter anymore. She was someone new. Someone who was determined not to let the world think her difficult.

Yet for all her determination, Tressa nearly turned back at the lichgate. Because if she had felt herself heartbroken before, she knew now she had been wrong. This was true heartbreak—this hideous rending pain that felt as if that absurd organ had cracked in two and was showering broken shards of glass within her chest at the last sight of her beloved bell tower, where she had spent hours and hours gazing out at the world, waiting for her chance to go out in it.

This *was* that chance, but she knew what she was about to do was irrevocable. She knew if she went with Matthew Kent now, there would be no coming back.

The temptation to stay—to keep safe and secure with everything the same was so strong, and so frightening, her fingers shook on the latch.

So, she forced her fingers off the gate, and the moment the latch clanged shut, she ran. She ran because that was what one did—one ran away. She clattered down the steep lane, cartwheeling her hands to keep her balance on the cold cobbles. She ran away from the past.

She ran away toward her future.

And there her future was, walking up from the quay. Matthew Kent was striding up the slope with his dark sea cape billowing behind him like a sail. Matthew Kent was smiling and reaching out his hand to catch her headlong flight. "I was on my way to get you. I wasn't sure you'd come."

"I told you—I'm not missish."

"And so you aren't. And I'm glad of it." He kissed her cold fingers and then laced his fingers with hers to lead her onward. "Come, let us away."

Together they ran down the long, curved length of the quay, and he kissed her hand again as if he could imbue her with his charming confidence before he set her aboard his ship. "You take the tiller, Teague," he ordered with a smile. "While I cast us off."

Tressa readily agreed—they should begin as they meant to go on.

She untied the line that had kept the tiller bowsed up securely, and then waited for Matthew to push the prow of the vessel away from the quay, until the bow caught the flow of the outgoing tide. Tressa threw the tiller wide, pivoting the vessel away from the stone quay. Another moment and Matthew had slipped the stern line and jumped aboard, going immediately forward to haul up the mainsail.

The dawn streaked up the coast just as they made the open water outside the harbor, and Tressa resisted the urge to look back, to take one last look at Bocka Morrow. But Matthew was hauling up the mizzen, and the dark, rusty-colored sails filled with wind, and the tiller took the bite of the water, and she had to concentrate on the water ahead—on what was next. She set a course, running full and by to the southwest.

"Regrets?" he asked as he came aft to lean against the taffrail.

"I don't believe in regrets." She smiled at him to mitigate the sting of the lie. "I've never been able to afford them."

He laughed merrily, just as she hoped he would. "I hope you never do afford them—they're a great waste of time."

It was as good a philosophy as any, as she was determined not to waste another minute of her time pretending to be anything other than she was. "Have you no regrets?" she asked. "I would have thought you regretted your decision to go against orders while blockading the Norwegian coast—"

"Damn, Teague, but you have a talent for finding out things a man doesn't want made known." He shoved a hand through his hair as if he were frustrated, but he was smiling as he looked away, checking the set of the sails. As if he admired her even as he damned her. "How did you learn that?"

"The information wasn't that hard to find," she admitted. "The incident was reported in the newspapers. You come from a famous family of Royal Navy captains—your father has been made a baronet in preference of his service to the crown—so it is only natural that your trials as well as your triumphs be noted."

"I much prefer the triumphs."

"Don't we all." Except in her life, the triumphs had never been trumpeted in a newspaper—nor even by her own family. They had been small, private moments of accomplishment—the first night she had kept track of the tots from a cargo, or when she had seen her suggestions for improving the distribution of the goods implemented. Or when she had helped Captain Kent rid Bocka Morrow of a traitor.

But if anyone besides her sister Nessa knew any of those things, Tressa would be greatly surprised.

Matthew Kent was thinking of more prosaic, practical things. "We'll sail for Falmouth and put into the Carrick Roads to find anchorage in the River Fal this night. With only two of us, I think it best not to stand watch on watch, but to overnight in protected anchorages."

Kent spared a look at the trim of the sails—he must have been satisfied with what he saw, because he didn't wait for her to answer, but ducked down the aft hatchway.

Tressa had never been below deck on the lugger—there had been no opportunity during the brief time she had been aboard during the fight against the French corvette—so she had no idea what sort of sleeping arrangements were to be made.

But she would not be missish—she had chosen this. She had chosen him. And when they had kissed it had been glorious.

She could only hope it would be again.

But Kent was not intent on being romantic—he returned

with a chart in his hand. "Tell me what you make of this." He unfurled a map showing the coast of France with the long cut of the canal to Gravelines. "I'll take the tiller for a spell."

Tressa knelt on the flat of the deck to study the chart. "Where did you get this?"

His smile lit the corners of his bright blue eyes with mischief. "From the corvette. I did have some small amount of forethought in thinking it might one day come in useful."

"Just so." She could feel herself returning his smile—he was impossible to resist when he was open and sunny and inviting. "These must be the fortifications the French prisoners mentioned"—the star-shaped outlines of fortified batteries were unmistakable, even to her—"on both sides of the canal at the mouth of the channel and here, closer to the old town itself. Vauban designed these in the last century if I'm not mistaken."

"You haven't been mistaken yet." His smile felt full of admiration, but he returned his attention to the ship and the tiller. "Tell me more."

"The rumors I heard in Guernsey are that warehouse is not within the fortifications—I believe it's here, along this deep canal they've dredged to accommodate ocean-going vessels."

"You've been to Guernsey? There's a vast deal more to you than meets the eye, isn't there, Teague?"

Not even his compliment could distract her, though it did warm her in the chill morning wind. "I shouldn't think you'd want to sail up that narrow, tidal canal—you'd be very easily trapped."

"Ah, but we won't mind the lugger being trapped—we want her to be. We will set her on fire and hope the flames we set will spread to other ships, as well as to the warehouses."

"Ah." Tressa pondered that requirement. "If we sail into

the canal, we have to pass the batteries before we set the fire, or they will surely try to sink us."

"Aye." He moved closer to stand just behind her, so he could look over her shoulder. "So, we'll have to time it precisely so the fire is large enough by the time the ship has reached these docks."

She followed the line of his pointing finger, letting speed and distance measure out in her mind. "Then we ought to be able to clear the batteries—they should take one look at your south coast-built lugger and take her for a smuggler." She pushed her thoughts in new directions. "What are the prevailing winds there?"

"I like the way you think, Teague." He rewarded her with a reassuring hand at her shoulder—a warm, confident squeeze that eased some of the tightness she didn't know she had in her neck. "Westerlies, which would not be so convenient, as they would blow the fire away from the warehouses. But I can lash the tiller wide at the last, to steer her for the docks."

"So, the problem is not how to get in, but how then to get out without a ship?" How to stay alive in the midst of such danger.

Tressa felt suddenly cold beneath her cloak, despite the strong winter sun warming the deck beneath her.

"Exactly, lass." Matthew's hand started kneading her shoulder in calm reassurance. "My brain is all for the main objective in setting the place afire, but I do realize a dead man can't collect medals or preferments or prize monies, and I should like to stay alive to receive at least one of them." His mischievous, devil-may-care laugh flew away with the wind. "So what say you, Teague? How shall we stay alive? For all I can think is that we'll have to learn to swim."

CHAPTER 11

"CAN YOU NOT SWIM?" She gaped at him as if he were mad. "And you on the water all your life?"

Matthew really did need to teach her to flirt. Or better yet, to swim—there was a world of sensual, slippery possibilities there. "Aye, lass, I was only joking."

Tressa let out an exasperated sigh. "I should hope so—in case you had forgotten, it is November, and we wouldn't last three minutes in that cold. I think we had far better use those fishing dories stacked on the foredeck instead—boats are a far more rational, far less lethal idea than swimming."

She shaded her eyes to look forward to the small boats in question, piled one atop the other like peas in a pod upon the deck. "And there appear to be enough of the dories to perhaps…"

Tendrils of her fine hair were blown in the wind, but his gaze was all for the fierce concentration on her face—it was as if he could see the wheels starting to turn faster, the gears meshing in her mind. "Aye? Go on," he encouraged her. "Impress me."

"A dory is the most practical and logical means of escape

—nothing simpler than to tail one off the stern of the lugger but…" She knelt back down at the chart, and measured the distance along the length of the canal with her fingers. "What we want to do is spread out the risk amongst the boats, and therefore increase the chances of success. That's what I do with the smuggling—divvy the cargoes into different boats and caves." She squinted at the map, as if she might make it come alive beneath her vision. "Do you know this coast? Is this stretch of beach inhabited?"

"Yes, I know it." He had done his turn at Channel duty, studying the coast of France through a spyglass for hours on end. "And no—it's empty dunes."

"The perfect place to hide a dory. Is this marsh behind?" She traced her way across the chart.

"Aye. With scrub and longer reeds than the grass on the dunes." He had never felt more attracted to her than at this moment when she was brilliant and beautiful all at the same time. He wanted nothing more than to take her in his arms—except that he also wanted her to keep saving his worthless neck.

"I think we ought to hide at least two of the dories along the coast here, one in the dunes, and another in the marsh, so we'll have two different avenues of escape."

"Excellent." He never would have thought of having a contingency—he would have simply sailed in by dead reckoning, improvising as he went and hoping to hell he wasn't out of his depth. But experience had taught him to understand the distance and time involved. "Although I'm worried about how long it might take to deploy two boats—we'll have to see if we can manage it just before twilight, because we'll need to make the canal of the L'Aa at fall of dark but at near high tide. The moon should be three-quarters full and waxing."

It was good to know he could come up with a few ideas she hadn't.

"Oh, yes. So we'll have some light reflecting off the sand of the dunes to mark the opening of the passage." She sat back on her haunches and looked to him. "What do you think? Do you think it will work?"

"I do, lass." Matthew could feel the certainty rise within him like the flames of the well-fueled fire he meant to set. "We'll make pyres in both the holds, well-soaked in lamp oil, but covered with tarpaulins over the combing to keep hidden until the moment. And then we'll becket the rudder—haul the tiller up tight with a rope to steer her to starboard—so that the bow goes into the dock and the stern swings wide, blocking the passage. And every sailor in the place will leap to their own vessels to try and save them, hopefully abandoning the warehouse to its own bad luck."

"Aye." Her smile was a reflection of their shared pleasure. "Indeed, that is exactly what Sally said happened in Brest—panic spread faster than the fire."

"And that is exactly what we want." Matthew could begin to see it all in his mind's eye—the hot flames, and the cold water, the chaos and confusion they would sow, the disruption to the enemy nation he had spent the whole of his life fighting.

He leaned back against the tiller and crossed his feet in satisfaction, as comfortable and pleased with the plan as he had ever been in the whole of his career. "Damn but you're bloody brilliant at this, Teague. Devil take me if you weren't born to it."

"Am I?" Her genuine surprise was a delight.

"You must have pirate blood in you, lass, running along with generations of smugglers' wiles. It's a miracle that you didn't take over the whole of the free trade while you were still in the cradle."

"I've a ways to go before I take over the whole of the trade, but I am nearly twenty. I hope there's still *some* time."

She was attempting to be light-hearted, but even if she was only twenty, she was an old soul, with those weary, seen-it-all-before, never restful eyes.

But something else about her pink-cheeked pleasure at his praise had him asking, "Has no one never told you that? Surely, they told you that in the caves? If you planned out the receipt of cargoes anything like you're planning this out, you're a bloody wonder."

"It's just what I do." She shrugged the compliment off. "There's no time for compliments, only for the job at hand. When I have the very livelihood of half the village in my responsibility, it's my job to get it right. No one ought to give me a compliment for that." She shook her head as if warding off the very idea. "If I wasn't good enough, I wouldn't get the job done."

The free traders of Bocka Morrow might not give her the compliments she was due, but he would. "You'd have made a hell of a sailor."

She gave him that sleepy, self-possessed smile that, for some reason he could not yet fathom, fired his blood. "I thought I *was* making a hell of a sailor."

"You are Tressa Teague, you are." He very nearly let the tiller go so he could pull her flush to his chest and kiss the bright exactitude from her lips.

But he did not. Instead, he held on to his rekindled admiration, enjoying the new sensation. He had never before felt something so…fraternal toward a woman. No, what he felt wasn't brotherly, but something more like camaraderie. Whatever it was, it was something he had never felt for a beautiful young woman he fancied.

It was an astonishing discovery—and he liked it. "I wonder what they'll make of you?"

"The French? I should hope I never find out what they would think of me. Oh, and we should put provisions—food and water at least—in the boats we hide if we mean to sail them back across the Channel."

"Agreed—we'll leave nothing on the lugger that we might need." Matthew laughed. He liked her wry sense of humor as well as the fact that she was always thinking—she couldn't seem to stop herself. "No—I meant what my family will think of you. Though I don't know which ones of them are at home at present, besides Grace and her children."

It was always something of a delight to come home to Cliff House and discover one or another of his brothers even temporarily in residence. "Grace keeps the home fires burning, as it were, while the rest of us come and go, on cruise and off."

"I know—or rather I know *of* Lady Grace from your sister's letters. But…" The unguarded animation stilled on Tressa's face. She turned away to look out over the bright water to the land passing under the larboard rail. "I should prefer not to meet them in Falmouth. I can't meet them now."

It was a simple enough statement, said without any rancor or petulance, but it struck him in a way it had not before—the precariousness of her position. She had left her family, and all her friends and had thrown herself in with him. And while their agreement might make all the sense in the word to the two of them, it would probably find no favor from the world at large.

Perhaps not even with his unconventional family.

"If you know Sally, you will know that she would be the last person to question your coming aboard with me. And after all your correspondence with her, she will be disappointed in me if I don't bring you to see her."

"Perhaps," she said, but her gaze, which had always met

his head-on, turned away over the sea. "When shall we reach Falmouth?"

"Before evening. Another six hours of easy sailing." The wind was high, the sky was bright, and the sun shone clear in the late autumn sky. There was nothing to blight their prospects—nothing but the worried frown pleating itself between her brows.

"You mustn't worry about them, Tressa," he assured her.

It was a pleasure to say her name, to allow himself the intimacy of that privilege. And it made him want other intimacies as well.

He reached for her hand and brought it to his lips. "We'll be fine, Tressa. I promise."

She finally laughed, but her bittersweet smile did him in. "Don't make promises you know you might not be able to keep, Kent. We neither of us know what the morrow will bring."

"It will bring victory." That was his captain voice, full of certain charm and confidence to inspire his men. But she was too smart to believe his bluster—she had already seen through his charm. "Listen to me, Tressa. I have always been happy to go to perdition quite comfortably all on my own, but I have never once led my men into a danger I didn't think they could face. But if this is a danger you don't think you can face, I will very gladly set you off safely in Falmouth until I can retrieve you."

Her answer was immediate. "Oh, no. You've got the danger all wrong, Kent. I don't mind the French at all." She pointed her face into the wind and closed her eyes. "It must be that pirate blood you accused me of having. I've made my choice, and I know what I'm doing."

Devil take him, he was glad of it.

Because he wasn't sure at all of what he was actually doing.

CHAPTER 12

MATTHEW KENT did something he had never done before—he let his heretofore unexercised scruples be his guide. For Tressa's sake, he reined in his strong impulse to visit his family, and instead, once they were anchored in the quiet shallows of the River Fal, satisfied himself in only rowing to Falmouth quay, and sending word—to be taken up to the house on the Cliff Road the next morning, after they had upped anchor and made their way eastward toward Portsmouth.

After it would be too late to stop them.

Yet, despite his uncharacteristic discretion—or perhaps because it was uncharacteristic—word reached Cliff House anyway, because no sooner had he purchased a hot pot of stew from a quayside alehouse and rowed back out to the lugger with his thoughts running more characteristically to the long, tall, brilliant, beautiful girl awaiting him below deck, than he was hailed from across the water.

"Ahoy, Kent!" It was his friend, former shipmate and brother-in-law David Colyear rowing out from the shore, mercifully alone.

"Col." Matthew greeted his friend, as he rowed alongside. "Good to see you, man."

"The same. Although I gather from this present mischief you're up to some ruse?"

Col knew him too well, but there was no profit in denying it. "Indeed."

Col gave him a meticulously assessing look. "Do I want to know about it?"

For a long moment, Matthew contemplated turning the whole of his plan over to Col, who was at least as meticulous a planner as Tressa Teague. And what a thing it would be to have Col by his side again—the plan would be assured of success were the man who had burned out Brest to come along. "I'm taking a page out of your book."

And Matthew's niggling scruple that he ought not put Tressa any closer to harm's way would be satisfied if he could trade her for Col. With Tressa safe with his family at Cliff House, he and Col could set the enemy aflame without a flicker of worry.

"I hope it's a different book—Sally is with child."

There was a horrible strained silence that rang in his ears—Matthew was sure he could not have heard his old friend aright. "My sister Sally?"

Col's stern mouth twisted up in a wry, one-sided smile. "Have you another sister I know nothing of?"

"No." Matthew knew he was gaping like a netted pilchard, wide-eyed and gasping for water. "But how—"

He would have thought his sister Sal the last woman on Earth who would want to have a child—she would have to give up sailing with her husband and live at Cliff House with Grace from now on.

"Well," Col said in his clam, wry way. "If you don't know how it's done by now, Matts, I'm afraid there's no hope for you."

But Matthew was too astonished to be embarrassed. "Col. Be serious. A baby?" Matthew's mind boggled with the implications.

"Yes. That's what we old married people seem to do—fall in love and be happy and have babies. Cliff house will soon be full of them, for Dominic's wife Georgiana is also due later this winter."

"Well, damn me." Matthew felt utterly becalmed, as if all the wind had run out of his sails. To be fair, it had been nearly six years since his bother and Georgiana had been married— nearly as long as Col and Sally. "I suppose the fairer question would be, what took you so long?"

"There *are* ways of planning these things, Matts," Col went on in his easy baritone. "But if you don't know that either, I really do fear for you out in the world." Col shook his head in mock sadness. "Time and tide wait for no man or woman—Sally's five and twenty now, and I am no longer by any stretch of the imagination a fresh-faced young lieutenant. But we've earned a fortune enough in prizes that we have the means to support a family now. So that's what we are doing." Col glanced back across the deck toward the small after-cabin. "As to what in hell *you* are doing, I reckon there are only two choices—either what you plan is illegal, unsavory, or dangerous. Or it involves a woman."

Matthew may have had his flaws, but generally, when he wasn't trying to root out traitors, lying wasn't amongst them. "All women are always dangerous."

Col let out a long low whistle. "God's balls, Matts, have you lost your mind?"

"I have not." He said it to convince himself as well as his friend. "I have a plan."

"You?" Col scoffed. "You've never made and kept a plan a day in your life."

"Don't act so shocked—I can plan things out you know."

With Col, Matthew couldn't always tell when his friend was taking the piss out of him.

But Col seemed serious. "Not in my experience."

"Come now." Matthew's pride objected. "I've been a Post captain nearly as long as you. I've learned from my experience."

"Your recent rebuke and reposting from the Admiralty said otherwise, though I hear from Grace and Owen that you are to be congratulated—that your time in the hinterlands of the west coast was well spent and ultimately successful. But why in hell you would want to jeopardize that success with a dubious scheme involving a woman?"

Because she wasn't just a woman.

There was nothing Matthew wanted more in that moment than to tell Col all—to tell him about Teague, and her plan, and pull out the chart and pore over the escape she had hatched—just so he could see the look of astonishment and admiration on Col's face.

But for the second time that evening, Matthew Kent thought beyond the small reach of this own needs and ambitions—to Tressa Teague's tenuous position. And to the risk that surely outweighed the reward for Col and his new family.

As little as Matthew liked the idea of putting Tressa in harm's way, he now liked putting Col there even less—to put Col at risk was also putting Sally and their baby in jeopardy.

And Matthew would not do that. "Don't worry yourself about me—it's just a jape, a bit of fun to impress a girl—a free trader," he added, lest his brother-in-law ask any other questions about the lass's identity that Matthew did not want to answer.

"A smuggler? You surprise me—I thought you were working against the free-traders and their law-breaking, revenue-dodging ways."

"I was working to root out a traitor and needed the smuggling confraternity's help. Her knowledge was invaluable, as it is for my next"—Matthew chose his word carefully—"mission."

"An official, Admiralty mission, or another foray against orders?"

"You know better than most that I would never purposefully go against orders." There was only so much abuse his pride, and his innate sense of duty, would withstand. But he didn't want Col to worry. "I'm just having a bit of fun before I return to Portsmouth and take up my command—I'm bound for the West Indies squadron."

"So I hear. And I congratulate you—your father's old command. You must be pleased."

"I am." Or at least he had been. Funny how he hadn't thought of that command in days.

Col held his oars for a long moment of silence. "I have to get back. I sneaked out, and if Sal finds I've gone off without her to meet you—which she will, because she's Sally Kent who has a nose for what goes on in a ship or a house or a town—and there will be the devil for me to pay."

Matthew clasped Col's hand. "A pleasure to see you, my friend."

"I wish it were more pleasure and less worry." Col shook his head. "Just promise me that you're not going to jeopardize your new command to impress a girl—a smuggler, for God's sake, who cannot be worth your effort."

"It's not like that, Col," Matthew said.

She wasn't like that.

And she was well worth any risk—even to his beloved career.

CHAPTER 13

*T*RESSA STAYED seated near the top of the companionway ladder until their conversation faded from earshot.

Just a ruse. A jape to impress a girl—a smuggler.

The words burned into her until she was so hot with the mortification of betrayal she couldn't breathe. She had believed he had been treating her as an equal. She had believed he was different. She had believed there was a special art of understanding between them.

She retreated to the small after-cabin, listening for the sound of his sea boots on the companionway ladder.

"Teague?" He smiled when he saw her. As if nothing were wrong. "I got us some stew from the quay, but I fear I've let it run cold."

She set herself to face him. "Having too much fun?" She could hear the scalded sarcasm that heated the edge of her voice to a rolling boil. "If you were trying to *impress me*, Kent, you've failed miserably."

He stilled, the way a smart man might when he sensed danger. "Oh, damn. What did I say?" But he held up a hand, as if he were mentally replaying his conversation in his head. "Damn me for an ass." He ran his hand through his hair as if that would help clear his obviously malfunctioning brain. "I didn't mean it in the way you think—I said that because I wanted to protect you—"

"I don't need your protection, Kent. I need your respect."

He stilled again, as if she had finally managed to shock him. "You have my respect. I would not be here—on this ship by your request, not up with my family at Cliff House—nor even contemplating this frankly dangerous ruse unless I had respect for your foresight and abilities."

This statement—along with the apparent sincerity in his voice—took some of the heat from her hurt. But not all.

She crossed her arms over her chest in the useless hope of holding the pain of disappointment within, of reasserting her faculties of reason to answer for the problem. But the problem was that she'd got her feelings hurt, and there wasn't much room for reason in that. "Then why did you not voice that respect to Captain Colyear? You purposefully misled him."

"Yes. Quite purposefully—you said you preferred not to meet them, so I purposefully did not say your name in case they recognized it. Even if Col didn't, both Sally and Grace surely would. But I understand now, how that might not seem respectful, but I meant my words to have the opposite effect. You have my apology—I can think as fast as the devil himself when I'm commanding a ship, but in affairs of the heart, I'm afraid I'm entirely an ass."

Tressa was sure she wanted to say something reasoned but could not—she had not really heard another word after *affairs of the heart*. "I— Thank you."

But he was not done with her—she had slighted him as well. "Respect goes hand in hand with trust, Tressa Teague." His voice was low and quiet and deeply personal. "And you have to decide right now, this night, whether you trust me, or not."

This was the most important thing he had ever said to her because it was also the truest—though she had needed him, and been charmed and attracted to him, she had never completely trusted him. "Can you give me any good reason why I should?"

"Yes." He was all determined seriousness. "Because there will be no medals or preferment or even mention of my name in Admiralty dispatches no matter how well or how badly we do on the morrow. Because the only thing that I will get from this misadventure—the only thing I want—is your company and the satisfaction of knowing that we did what we set out to do. Do you understand?"

"Not exactly." He was overthrowing every conception she had made about him. She understood and respected his ambitions. For him to foreswear those ambitions now, made no sense to her.

"This adventure is ours, and ours alone. The Admiralty will never know I was involved even if we do manage to burn down half of France."

"Then why are you doing it?" Her heart and her pride—all of her hopes—rested upon his answer.

"Because your idea was good, and worthy—too worthy to disregard. And because the things I value more than anything else are loyalty and friendship. You gave me both of those things, and I aim to pay you back in kind."

The struggle between her heart and her pride was excruciating. "What you feel for me is but loyalty and friendship?"

"No buts about it." He spoke solemnly. "My heart beats true, Tressa Teague. If you stay true to me, I will be true to you."

Ah, but for that to happen, she could have to have the courage to be true to herself.

The moment stretched out too long without her answer.

Matthew tried to smile over his frown but gestured to the wall of four curtained bunks set into the stern. "Best get some rest. You'll need it in the morning."

And he disappeared back up the ladder.

She was still awake, still wearing all of her clothes though she was in one of the bunks, staring into the dark behind her curtain, when he finally returned below deck. She listened to the small rustling sounds that signaled he was disrobing—the slide of fabric across his shoulders, and muted staccato of buttons popping free, and the heavy clunk as boots were levered off.

Tressa's breath stopped up hot in her chest as she waited for him to push the curtain over, or press his weight into the thin cotton mattress, or speak her name again.

But none of those things happened—instead she heard him climb into his own bunk and settle himself in on the other side of the thin wall.

And she was left staring into the darkness, wondering if she really had got him all wrong—whether he was there only for the glory.

Or whether she was there only for the money.

Morning came before she had fully made up her mind.

In the dark before the dawn, Matthew was up, rapping on the wooden partition between their bunks. "Out and down, Teague. Show a leg and roust out."

Tressa came abruptly awake and drew back enough of the short curtains to find him already up and shoving his feet into sea boots and thrusting his arms into the sleeves of his sea coat by the light of a single lantern.

"Well, damn my eyes if you need any more beauty sleep, Tressa Teague—if you get any more beautiful, I'll go blind." He rubbed his hand across his face as if he could chafe some clarity into his eyes before he stood and faced her. "Well, what's it going to be?"

Tressa didn't pretend to misunderstand the question. She unfolded herself from the bunk as elegantly as possible—which was probably not the least bit elegantly at all. And though her mouth felt dry and full of cotton, and her heart was hammering in her chest like a church bell, she made her decision. "I'll stay. I want to stay."

"You're sure?" He came forward in the lamp light so she could see the glint in his eyes— the pleasure and satisfaction he did not otherwise show. "There can be no doubts, no mistrust from here on out, Tressa. We have to be able to rely upon each other without question."

She was back to being Tressa to him. That was enough for now. "Aye."

It was as if she had lit the wick of his merry charm. "Then I need you on deck within five minutes to up anchor, my Teague." He tossed her a smile and started up the companionway. "Extra points if you know how to make coffee."

"I don't. I'm not in the least bit domestic. But I brought apples with me for breakfast."

His answer was a laugh that warmed her in a way her heavy cloak could not. "Devil take me if I ever want you to be." He reached down to hand her up the stairs, and take a great chomping bite of the apple. "Pendragon red. Ought I to ask if it's enchanted?"

It was her turn to laugh. "It's only enchanted if you believe."

"And what do you believe?"

"That we make our own fates if we but have the courage to do so."

He kissed her hand. "Then come stand to the tiller, my courageous friend, and make your fate by letting her into the wind as she bears." And with one last glittering glance, he disappeared forward to see to the anchor.

As soon as they were out into deep water and making way up-channel with the sails set to catch the brisk following wind, Matthew came aft. "I'd forgotten what a pleasure it is to sail so simply—to feel the pull of the sheets beneath my own hands instead of standing on the quarterdeck calling out orders."

"The burden of being the captain—all the responsibility and none of the pleasure?"

His laugh was infectious. "You understand me perfectly. Though I'm sure my crews think a captain's job is nothing but pleasure. And they would be right if they could see me now, mid-channel on such a day, with the wind blowing thirty knots for France with a pretty lass by my side." He checked the lay of the sails, taking the gauge of the wind whipping them eastward. "We'll make Calais this day, if I'm any judge." He turned back to her. "Still no regrets?"

"I only regret that I mistrusted you."

She surprised him—his brows rose and his eyes widened before he quickly turned to humor. "I have great hopes that I can prove myself yet. And to do so, I'd best set to work."

As there were only two of them, Tressa's work—staying at the tiller and keeping them resolutely sailing east by northeast—was the far easier. Matthew bore the full brunt of the effort to amass every single piece of tinder or fuel that wasn't integral to the hull and pile it into the two forward holds that normally held nothing but nets and pilchards.

He came aft now and again to check with her and eat the bread and cheese she had provisioned. "I'll be glad enough to set this tub on fire. I don't think I'll ever get the stink of pilchards out of my nose, no matter how the men scrubbed and holystoned the hell out of those holds."

Tressa had to laugh at such fastidiousness from such a

man—the sturdy sea coat he was wearing against the chill wind must have been old and used the first time he put it on. "This ship hardly smells at all, but I suppose I've become inured to the stink of fish—I've lived within whiffing distance of the quay and the pilchards all my life."

He had no objections to such a low situation. "You're a rare lass, Teague."

And he was a rarer man, still. How many other men of her acquaintance or experience would have asked, let alone agreed to take her on? How many decorated frigate captains would be happy to have someone like her—a woman and a smuggler—pilot them up-channel? How many men would have agreed to give up a sizable portion of their prize money without being asked?

Not that she didn't think she deserved the payment—and she was certainly earning that money all over again by going on with him now. But she was also getting the adventure and the control she had always craved—for the first time in her life, she felt as if she were very much in charge of her own fate.

She had could only hope the French cannon weren't going to change that.

CHAPTER 14

TRESSA HAD TOLD HIM twice that she had no regrets, but she was wrong—regret hit her hard in the chest the moment the mouth of the canal of Gravelines gaped at them like a black maw between the ghostly white of the moonlight off the dunes.

She should never have suggested this scheme.

She should never have come with him to carry it out.

She should never have thought she was brave enough for such a thing. Because this night, she might well and truly die, and the thing she regretted the most was that she had not spent the past two nights making mad, passionate love to Matthew Kent.

And it was too late now. She was committed.

"Point her dead in, Teague, and hold steady as she goes."

Tressa swallowed the misgivings that were lodged like a hot stone in her throat and nodded. "Aye."

She peered hard at the sliver of dark that rose and fell between the bow rail and the jib above and gripped the tiller until her knuckles shone white against the polished wood.

This was what she had wanted—responsibility, equality, and above all, respect.

They had already made all the arrangements they possibly might before they had run out of time—they had only been able to hide one dory in the dunes before the early winter sunset had made it too dark to chance any further landings. The distances that had looked so conquerable on a map had proved daunting in reality.

Matthew had already lowered the spanker sail aft, leaving it slack against the deck where it would serve as fuel to feed the fire, and was trimming the other sails, adjusting them to the changing wind direction as the lugger passed into the lee of the land.

"Good lass." He called encouragement from amidships. "Steady on. Coming in nicely. Eyes ahead on the unfamiliar way up the canal, while I look busy at the sails. That's it."

He let out more slack so the ship slowed, just as it ought, as they passed through the dunes and under the loom of the dual fortifications of Fort St. Philippe.

It felt as if a hundred pairs of eyes must be looking down at them, weighing out the cut of their rig, sizing her up in a spyglass. Tressa's heart was hammering like a church bell inside her chest, and she felt hot and cold all at the same time as a fine sheen of perspiration broke out along the line of her spine under the sturdy wool of her gown, chilling her to the bone.

She calmed herself as she always had during a smuggling run—by going over the plan in her head. She would keep to her station until they were in sight of the warehouse, whereupon Matthew would throw back the tarpaulins covering the hold, light the pyre, and come take the tiller while she went into the dory tailed off the stern, stepping the mast while he tied off the tiller before joining her.

What came after that would be improvisation and

making the most of the circumstances as they happened—something he had considerably more experience with than she did.

But what came next was entirely unexpected—Matthew ran back to her, his blue eyes dark and shining under the moon. "New plan." He started working a rope around the bulwark to becket the tiller and hold it steady so she didn't have to. "I'm putting you off."

He grabbed her upper arm and hauled her toward the taffrail. "Now."

"No," she objected immediately. "I can do—"

He hustled her to the rail, implacable. "The channel is too narrow. You're taking the dory and heading to the marsh now, do you understand?"

"No." She could not go off without him. She had no talent for improvisation. Without the plan to follow, she would be —to use an unfortunate phrase—dead in the water.

It was as if he didn't hear her. "Row for the marsh immediately," he ordered. "Hide there, and I will meet you."

Her fingers were losing their grip under his stronger pressure. "When?"

"Wait no longer than daylight. Judge for yourself whether to row out of the marsh or head across to the dune to take the other boat across the channel. But no longer than daylight."

He all but tossed her over the taffrail, and she clambered into the boat tailed off the stern, trying to gain her balance and still hold on to his hand as if it were a lifeline. "But what about you?"

His face was shadowed above her. "Daylight, do you hear? Promise me." He gripped her arm hard, as if he were prepared to shake the oath from her if need be.

She had never been so terrified in all her life. "I promise."

His relief was audible. "I love you."

She could not have been more shocked if he had thrown her into the icy water—everything within her was a turmoil of hot and cold all at the same time. A painful, glorious lump rose in her throat, stopping her speech.

Tressa had understood that he was attracted to her and even admired her. But love—love was more than she had hoped. And certainly more than she had bargained for, though her heart swooped and sang like a lark at break of day.

But there was no time to say anything—he let her go, pushing her away, yanking the painter free, and she was alone in the stern of the dory, watching the lugger sail away down the canal.

Dead in the water.

And hoping to heaven he wasn't planning to become the same.

MATTHEW'S RELIEF was a physical thing—an easing in his chest that allowed him to breathe freely. Now that he knew she was safe, he could finish what she had so capably started without regard for what happened next. Now that he had spoken, he could face whatever danger lay ahead with a clear conscience and a clean heart.

It had all started to go too fast. He had expected the strange feeling of speed—he had been through enough battles to know that time was a strange beast, as fickle and untamable as a bumblebee, alighting one moment and flitting on in the next.

But it had never felt so out-of-the ordinary before, as if the bees might sting him to death before he could accomplish what they had set out from Bocka Morrow to do.

But all *he* had really set out to do was get the girl.

Matthew forced all thoughts of strange, nonsensical girls and bumblebees from his head—he had to put the flame to the readied pyre. He threw the lit lantern down into the hold, letting it crash and splatter to catch the oil-soaked rags stuffed amongst the hempen ropes and wooden furniture and torn-up deck fittings, before he ran back to the let the mainsail down just enough so the foot of the sail dangled down into the flames, adding the dark canvas as fuel to the fire.

And then the wind caught the flames pushing them up the canvas, spreading the flickering destruction climbing the mast and dancing down lines. The fire grew, blossoming out from amidships like a greedy orange flower, consuming the foredeck.

Around him the air turned hot and gusty—the fire making its own wind, the flames pulling the air into the vortex of heat and light. That wind blew into the foresail, pushing the lugger faster until the flames leap across the divide and began to lick at the foresail and jib.

A cry went up from somewhere ahead. "*Au feu!*"

Figures started to appear at the side of the canal as the light from spreading fire illuminated the quay. The dock ahead was crowded with a cluster of ships, and Matthew aimed hard for their dark hulls, waiting until the last possible moment, when the lugger began losing headway, before he pushed the tiller wide, spinning the little ship so she would ram headlong into the small space between two larger vessels, waiting to make sure, bracing for her blunt bow to smash into the stone and wood of the wharf.

The impact of the crash pitched him forward at the same time that the charred, smoking mainmast was cast forward to land on the hidden but loaded, forward guns in a shower of splintering spark.

Before he could brace himself a second time, the guns

fired off, exploding one right after the other, blowing a path of death and destruction into the warehouse.

Around him the world erupted into flame.

And Matthew did the first sensible thing he had done in days—he pitched himself headlong over the side and into the sea.

CHAPTER 15

HE CAME UP sputtering and gasping in the frigid air, already half numb with the cold—the icy water cut through his chest like a knife, making it painful to breathe.

Matthew struck out for the opposite bank of the canal, which was darker and less inhabited, though the larger of the two forts was on that side. No matter, for behind him all was shouts and confusion as crews were rallied to fight the fire as sparks rained through the air.

The sparks were immediately followed by the crack of a gunshot—the water ahead of him flew upwards in a spout.

Experience pushed him under, diving as deep as he dared, to stay safe from the shot while he tried to gauge his direction through the water. But the cold made his lungs grow tight and hard with the effort to swim as far as he could before he was forced to the surface again.

Another cracking gunshot and he dove, trying to stroke in a different direction to confuse the enemy shooter, north along the canal, but in the dark murk of the water he could not be sure of his way. His hands hit mud, and he was forced upward again to find himself within yards of the bank—the dockside bank.

A volley of shots had him throwing himself back under the inadequate protection of the freezing water once more. But in the all too brief time he had been gulping in air, he had glimpsed the wooden pilings that buttressed the embankment above. He might be safe there out of gunshot range—enough to catch his breath and decide what to do next before the structure might catch fire and collapse above him.

And generally, it were best if he were on the same side of the canal as Tressa and the marsh. And while he knew without a doubt his current situation could not in any way be called a good plan, he was sanguine with the knowledge that had Tressa and the boat still been with him, they would have been shot out of the water.

He might be still.

It was getting harder to swim, harder to make his body move in the cold. Harder to think rationally—not that he had ever been any great shakes at rational thought. But he knew enough now in the small animal part of his brain that he needed to go to cover, to get out of the heat-sapping water and move his body to keep himself warm.

He crawled beneath the embankment, clambering onto a slanted piling to get himself above the sucking mud, to hide in the dark, beyond the reach of the orange shimmer of light reflecting over the water. But even under the embankment, and only a hundred yards from a blazing hot fire, the wind seemed to slice through his wet wool clothing. If he didn't get dry and out of the wind, he was going to have a bloody hard time of it.

He listened for a few short moments as the conflagration some small ways down the canal seemed to grow—he could hear the snapping and crackling of the flames and smell the bitter stink of ash on the wind. He could also hear the cries and pounding of feet on the wooden planking above, as men rushed to and fro.

Out in the middle of the canal a raft of other smaller boats were attempting to make their way around the stern of the flaming lugger before the tide stranded them on the other side. Perhaps in the confusion he might be able to make it out to one of them, and hope they were an English crew.

And then there was one boat, apart from the others sailing into the teeth of the exodus. A boat piloted by one long, tall, disobedient girl.

"Tressa." He croaked her name as he flung himself back into the icy water and tried to make his way toward her. But she sailed on, and he had overdrawn his strength.

"Teague." He couldn't follow her, and when he turned to go back under the pilings, feared he wouldn't make it either.

Devil take him if he were going to drown within eight feet of the damn bank. No matter if his legs felt leaden, and the wool of his clothing grew heavier and heavier, pulling him down. He would make it. He would take it slow and easy and float if he had to rest.

And then his head was jerked back, his hair tangled in some unseen snag.

He reached back—

"Stop struggling," a voice hissed, as it hauled him up by the hair. "Give me your hand."

It was his Tressa, thank the devil, white as a sheet, her face drawn and set as she dragged him over the counter of the little dory like a beached dolphin, flopping and gasping at her feet.

"Stay down." She threw a heavy woolen blanket over him. And he felt something else drape against his back—netting, he supposed from the pilchard harvest.

And there was nothing he could do but gasp and shiver and curl around the skinny warmth of her legs and ankles and wait for her to take them to some sort of safety.

And set himself to still be alive when she did.

Oh, heaven help her, but his hands were ice cold where they tried to grasp her ankles. If Tressa had been frightened before, she was utterly terrified now. And she had never felt so alone, even with Matthew safely hidden in the bottom of the boat.

She could feel his shivered convulsions and was half afraid the men in the nearby boats making their escape up the canal could see the blanket move. She did what she could to camouflage the wet heap of man curled at her feet—shifting her cloak to fall a certain way and pulling some of the netting from the sternsheets bench where it had been stowed.

And thank heavens there had been an old woolen blanket under the pile of netting—the bulk of the provisions she had planned for the dories were in the boat still hopefully hidden in the dunes. Which was where they had best go—she had no confidence in her ability to pilot them across the channel in an open boat at this time of night. The wind had shifted, blowing cold out of the northeast—a frigid Baltic storm would soon be upon them.

On second thought, the marsh would be more protected. The vast majority of the other boats scuttling about the canal were hauling up on the mud and sands on the opposite bank, well away from both the fire and any need to help fight it—each for their own safety under fire.

Tressa kept her hood up to cover her blond head and steered in the wake of a boat still bearing out of the canal, but as soon as they had passed beneath the scrutiny of the entry forts, she set the dory skimming across the shallows that wound through the tidal marsh, finding shelter and cover in the tall reeds.

It grew harder to make her way as the storm clouds passed across the moon, so all she could do was aim up a narrow ribbon of water that cut through the reeds, leading to a dark thicket of scrub trees.

"Matthew?" She touched the blanket at her feet. "You can come out now. We've made cover in the marsh."

"Good lass." He sounded drunk or sleepy, fumbling a little as he came up from under the blanket. "I should help you."

"You can barely stand." And no wonder—his fingers and skin where she touched him were white with the chill. Tressa had to prop herself under his arms to hoist him out of the boat.

"Give me a minute, lass," he said again as his exhausted exhalation curled in the cold air above his head. "Keep me moving for a bit to get me warmed up."

"Only to the thicket." Her own breath came out in a stream of steam from the exertion of his weight as they made their way up to a thicket of scrub pine, long grass and brush. "I have to get the boat."

"Tide's on the ebb. It'll be fine," he panted through wreaths of breath.

"No. I want it for a shelter—it looks to storm. You hunker down here." She set him with his back to the dune, so he was out of the wind. "Rub your arms as best you can to get your blood flowing. We'll get you dry as soon as we can." But exactly how, when the only shelter they were like to get from the coming storm was an overturned dory wedged amongst the scrub, she wasn't exactly sure.

For her own part, Tressa was soon growing too warm beneath her clothes from the exertion of hauling the dory up the short incline to the thicket and inverting it to form a crude shelter. "Here." She wrapped her cloak around Matthew instead—it would do him more good. "With your ginger hair, you'll look quite fetching in green."

His devil-may-care smile answered before his chattered words. "One tries one's best."

"Try your best to crawl on in there, while I cover up our tracks."

"You do that. Though I can't think,"—he was regaining his strength with every word— "anyone would trace us here. We've done well, Teague. I'm enjoying the view."

She followed his gaze far across the marsh and the widening sand of the beach to the low city where the flames could be seen leaping high into the night.

"That sight warms me as well as any fireplace," he lied on a happy, shivered sigh.

It was all bravado of course, but Tressa wasn't about to argue with him—she was too busy thinking and making contingencies and gauging the moment when the storm might break. The air crackled with more than just the sounds of the fire—off to the northeast flashes of lightning lit the night sky.

She broke off a branch of scrub pine to erase as best she could the line of the dory's keel through the sand, though if the rain came as she feared, all traces of their passage would soon be mercifully obliterated.

She returned up the short incline of the dune to find Matthew had clambered to his feet and was stripping off his soaking wet clothing.

"Here," she dropped the branch, and stood behind him, holding up the old wool blanket to shield him from the wind. "Give the wet things to me and take the blanket when you're done."

"I will if it won't offend your delicate missish sensibilities."

If he could laugh in the face of such peril, so could she.

"Why don't you do it anyway, Kent, and we'll see just how delicate my sensibilities are."

CHAPTER 16

HE HAD OFTEN, in the past month, dreamed of Tressa Teague undressing him. But in those delightful imaginings he had not been pale white and shivering like a ginger-topped icicle.

The only thing to do in such an undignified position was laugh at himself, and hope she laughed along.

Matthew clumsily toed off his boots and peeled down to his small clothes, before he chaffed himself dry with the rough wool blanket. Beside him, Teague never batted a lash, as efficient as a valet, wringing as much icy water as she could from his sopping coat, breeches and stockings.

"I'd hang them out to dry for a bit in this wind, but I've no confidence that the rain will hold off for any more than a few minutes longer." She gathered the clothes and picked up the branch of scrubby pine. "I'll pull this in behind us to cover our way. Will that do, do you suppose?"

"Aye." He was already warmer without the chilling wet of his clothing—warm and steady enough put his nose to the wind. "I fear you're right about the rain."

In an effort to preserve whatever dignity, or masculinity,

remained to him, Matthew did the gentlemanly thing, and after he had covered himself with the blanket, he handed Tressa back her cloak. "Let us get out of this wind." He gestured for her to precede him beneath the overturned dory.

They had both crouched down to enter when voices came to them on the wind.

Tressa froze, listening, and they turned together to see a dot of light—a lantern—bobbing, as if on a boat making its way through the murky marsh. "Soldiers."

"Get in," he ordered, taking the branch from her hands. The instinct to act, to reach for the sword he seemed to have lost in the water, heated his blood more effectively than a bonfire. "Hand me out the gun that should be in the sternsheets."

He took the weapon she so efficiently found, but in his position, discretion was surely the better part of valor—better to hide and live to fight another day that to be taken near naked and shivering.

Matthew inched his way under the cover backward, using the brush to hastily sweep their footprints from the sand. But just as he was positioning the piece of brush to better camouflage their hiding spot, he heard the distinctive patter of raindrops against the overturned hull of the dory.

"Rain," he whispered unnecessarily, into the dark of their little space.

Or perhaps more necessarily than he thought—Tressa exhaled as if she had been holding her breath. "Thank God."

Matthew wasn't quite ready to thank the deity. "It'll put paid to the fire." Still they had done as much as they could—they had sowed destruction and confusion amongst the enemy, and in so doing and accomplished what they had set out to do.

Mostly.

He said no more but listened, accustoming his tall spine to the space, squashed together with her under the sloping roof of the dory, straining to hear the snatches of the soldiers' conversations carried to them on the wind, only to be drowned out by a crack of thunder that shook the boat, and made Tressa gasp and reach for him in the dark.

He kept hold of her hand. "They'll go back," he assured her in a low murmur. "I'm sure they had much rather spend the night in a dry barracks than a wet shore." He let his eager finger follow the line of her arm to her shoulder so he could gather her to him. "We will be saved by the selfish nature of men everywhere, who would rather see to their comfort than their duty."

His own comfort was greatly augmented by wrapping the blanket around the two of them together—he warmed by degrees with her lithe torso pressed against his.

But just when he though his naturally hale animal imperviousness to weather had begun to reassert itself, Tressa began shivering. "I'm making you cold." He started to slide his arm from her shoulder.

"No." She rewrapped herself around his middle. "I'm not cold, really. Just…" Her shivered whisper vibrated with emotion in the dark. "Overwhelmed, I suppose."

He heard the fright behind the carefully chosen word, and he understood—he remembered his first brushes with the danger of battle far too well. Those memories, and others he could never hope to forget, would stay with him always.

And she had been so calm, so steady, so resolute—not only this night, but that night at Black Cove in Bocka Morrow—that he could only admire her resolve in holding her feelings in check for so long.

He found her forehead to kiss. "The terror can take some like that, after the danger has passed. You've done a fine job of keeping it all in, but it has all got to shake its way out. You just let it do so, and you'll be fine in a moment."

"I didn't think I was afraid. Not for myself. But I was terrified that I had lost you."

This he also understood—it was the whole of the reason he had so abruptly put her off the lugger.

But he was also inordinately pleased that her thoughts had all been for him. "Me?" He wrapped his arm around her and pulled her tight against his side. "Don't you know you never have to worry about me—for I've the devil's own luck. Everyone says so."

"You nearly drowned. And you're still as cold as a block of ice."

"Not quite—I'm warming. You're warming me." He let his hands explore the outline of her head—her chin and face and soft, spilling hair.

"You were under that freezing water for a horribly long time. And all the while the fire was blazing up, and someone started shooting and everyone ran in a hundred different directions. I've never seen the like in all my life."

She had to have been far nearer than he thought, to have seen all that. "You're not very good at obeying orders."

She made a rude sound of objection. "How else was I to find you? If you are lucky, you're lucky that I found you when I did."

"So I am." His finger stroked the long line of her jaw. "And not a moment too soon." He found her lips and kissed her in thanks.

She instantly pressed herself to him, kissing him back.

He was immediately suffused with heat—the heat of desire and want. The heat of life—in the face of danger they would celebrate being alive and together. "Tressa."

No matter that he had called her Teague and talked to her as if she were his lieutenant. No matter that she done better for him than many a lieutenant could. She was not a lieutenant—she was a woman. His woman. "I want you. And I mean to have you now, if you'll—"

She cut off his words with her eager lips upon his.

She gripped the edge of the blanket and levered herself against him, angling her mouth to his, offering him her body without preface. Without condition.

She kissed him ardently, pressing her lips against his, then shifting to kiss her way along the rough line of his whiskered jaw. And then she came back with her lips upon his, kissing until she was opening her mouth and delving in to taste him.

And then her hands were no longer on the blanket, but around his neck and in his hair, holding him still and near, so she could whisper in his ear. "Yes. Please."

Triumph surged anew through his blood. But he had been rash and impulsive enough for a lifetime—she was too important to rush. "Are you sure?"

"I am," was her immediate response. "I want to be with you. Please." She kissed the very edge of his ear. "If I could have this one chance to be with you, it will be all I ask."

"Tressa." As if she had to convince him. As if he weren't already determined upon the very same thing. "I told you once before that my heart beats true. You've been true to me, and I will be true to you."

CHAPTER 17

Matthew held her for such a long time, his bright eyes glittering but unfathomable in the velvet dark, roaming over her face as if she were a chart he might memorize. And then his finger followed the path of his gaze, carefully outlining each and every curve and plane, brushing lightly over her lashes, skimming along the outline of her lips.

Tressa couldn't stand the tender scrutiny. "Please." She pressed her mouth into the hollow of his throat where his pulse beat strong and steady beneath her lips.

His arms tightened around her back to draw her hard against his chest. His kiss delved into her mouth, and let his hands roam over her back, until they came up to rake through her hair, cradling her jaw, and holding her still for a hot, heartfelt kiss.

"Yes," she gasped in encouragement. She wanted the blistering heat that began to pulse through her veins, warming her enough to drive out the chill of uncertainty.

He pulled away to look down at her for another long moment, while his hand came back up to stroke her cheek and cradle her jaw, as if to tell her there was no rush. "We've all the time in the world."

He was wrong, of course. They had so little time—they were still in danger, hiding on an enemy shore, unsure of what the morrow might bring. But she placed her hands over his and tipped her head, leaning her cheek into his hand. Resting there, safe in his arms for a blissful moment, until he leaned away, letting go of her.

He spread the woolen blanket over the sand before he took her into his arms carefully, reverently, as if she were as fragile as a teacup, and not a tall tankard of a girl.

But it was as if he could read her mind. "You are a tall drink of water, Tressa Teague. And I'm parched for the taste of you."

He tasted of brandy and warmth and strength. She gave herself up to the kiss, using her lips and tongue to explore the wonder of him, to become one with him, body and soul. To draw him ever nearer, so that even as they kissed, her fingers could explore the broad contours of his shoulders and chest.

Matthew returned the service, loosening the tie of her cloak and tossing it aside before he took her by the upper arms and began to ease the sleeves of her plain woolen dress from her shoulders.

"You're sure?" he asked quietly, as he dropped a kiss on the skin of her shoulder.

"Yes." There was no other answer. She wouldn't allow there to be.

"Long, tall Tressa Teague." He laid her down upon the blanket before he stretched out next to her, drawing her torso flush with his, letting his hands skim lightly over the length of her body, up and down her arms, around her face and into her hair. Each touch, each whisper of his breath along her skin, wound down through her belly until the sweet tension coiled throughout her body.

He speared his fingers through her hair, unraveling her messy braid and spreading the long strands out around her head. He buried his face in it, inhaling deeply.

Which for some reason made her smile into the dark. "I'm sure I smell of gunpowder and tar."

"You smell of danger and excitement," he countered at her ear. "And you taste of—" He kissed her deeply. "You taste of cleverness and loyalty, which is the sweetest taste there is."

She could only smile at so silly and so sweet a comparison. "Better than brandy?"

His fingers traced the contour of her lips. "Better than everything."

He was so tender under all that brash, careless charm. She thought he might say something else, but after a long moment he simply closed his eyes and breathed deeply, before he kissed her again, with slower, more careful kisses, taking his time and relaxing into her embrace. Tressa's eyes fluttered closed as she gave herself over to the pleasure. Matthew's hands heated her wherever they touched, gliding over the curve of her hip and smoothing down and around her bottom.

His lips were at her ear, even as his hands cupped her, the words the same evocative murmur. "My sweet Tressa. So true."

She needed little else to inflame her—the heat of his hands, the touch of his tongue at her ear, all set the inexorable tide of passion rising within her. She felt the strong bone structure of his handsome face beneath her palms, the strength of his passion for life. And for her.

She was not so naive as to think she was the only woman he had ever loved, but she was the woman he was loving now. He was magnificent, with his blazing red hair and deep blue eyes. He was the man *she* had chosen—and was choosing now.

Tressa ran her fingers up the sides of his temples to trace the faint lines of his scowl, so familiar and dear to her now. Her hands delved into his windswept hair, traced the shape of his skull, and down the strong cords of muscles in his neck as she pulled herself back up to his mouth.

She wanted to be closer, to discover everything there was to know about him. She slanted her mouth across his, deepening the kiss. She wanted and needed to feel the heat of his skin next to hers, to feel the comforting strength of his body wrap around her. To choose her. To need her.

When their tongues met and tangled in her mouth, Tessa gasped aloud with the sheer joy of the sensations streaking across her skin like lightning. Even her hands felt hot and tingly as she ran them over his body, so different from her own. His skin was warming and inviting, his chest was sprinkled with hair that lightly abraded the sensitive tips of her fingers and palms.

Her breathing shifted into audible pants that should have embarrassed her, but she was beyond embarrassment, beyond even the recall of reason.

Matthew was here, with her, and she would have him now. Now, before anything or anyone else could come between them, or stop them. She would have this one perfect night, so she could live off its memory for years to come.

Tressa trailed her hands down his long torso, to the edge of his damp small clothes, growing anxious to hurry him along.

"I should have shucked those despite your delicate sensibilities," he growled as he levered himself off her. "We both should have. Come."

He came onto his knees beside her. "I want to undress you properly. And make love to you properly with the morning light streaming through the stern gallery, lighting up your skin. But this will do just as well. Even better."

She had nothing left of modesty—she went straight to the ties at his waist, grazing her fingers across the growing bulge at the apex of his thighs.

"Handsomely, now, Teague," he murmured, on a low laugh, covering her hands with his own, and guiding her hands to clasp him firmly. "Slowly, love. We have all night."

"We do not," she contradicted him on a kiss. "We may be discovered at any moment."

"Then we had best be very, very quiet while we bring each other to perfect ecstasy."

Ecstasy—it sounded like a faraway island she would never find without a map. She wished in that moment for a map of his body, a topographical study of the intriguing ridge of muscle that ran along his hips and disappeared beneath his breeches.

She slid her hands down along the muscled path to the button flap, and he growled, "You are a curious lass, aren't you?" He kissed her again. "I like curious. I like naked and curious even better."

He illustrated his delightful point by undoing the buttons at the back of her dress, and helping the fabric to fall with a *shush* to her waist. "Better," he whispered as he traced the sensitive undersides of her breasts before his hands settled to untie her front-lacing stays. "And better still. So practical and well-reasoned, Teague."

She smiled even as she kissed him—he would make her laugh even as he made love.

Tressa helped him along, shimmying out of the stays before she reached for the bottom of her shift and shucked it over her head without a moment of consciousness.

"Best." He brushed his palm lightly across her tight

nipples, first one breast and then the other, until she felt her flesh contract into an almost painful burst of bliss.

She gasped and arched her back, pressing herself forward into his hands, even as she put her own hands to work. "Now you. Because I think I'm going to like naked, too."

CHAPTER 18

SHE WAS SUCH a woman for him—making him laugh even as she made his cock press heedlessly against the thin cover of his small clothes. He wanted this marvelous girl so badly, he hoped to hell he could shuck them off in time. He had anticipated a slow seduction, but devil take him if she wasn't his equal in this as in all things.

"Handsomely now," he murmured again, but she liked her own way, and the moment he had pushed his small clothes clear of his hips, she had him in hand.

He used his groan of satisfaction to run the edge of his tongue lightly across the sweet peak of her nipple, wetting the lovely tight bud before he abruptly nipped, abrading the sensitive flesh against the sharp edge of his teeth.

She cried out in pleasure, her eyes clenched shut tight to absorb the intense sensation, so he rasped the other peak while his hand dove down across the sleek scoop of her belly and into the nest of soft curls between her soft thighs. "And there is best of all."

He covered her gasp with his mouth, taking pleasure in

the breathy sounds of pleasure that rose with each shallow, rapid inhale.

He lifted her with one hand around her back, setting her gloriously long legs to wrap around his waist, wreathing him in the scent and feel of her. She held him tight, as if he were the only solid thing in a sea of flotsam.

Matthew tumbled them onto the blanket and rose over her, running his free hand all the way down her endless legs, kneading the straining muscles rhythmically until she caught the rhythm and began to move her hips in time, riding his hand as it covered her mound.

"Handsomely *now*." He slowly slid one long finger inside and felt her inner muscles close around him, hot and slick and delicious. She was close—so close he could feel her pulsating.

God's balls. Matthew sent up the blasphemous prayer as he leaned over her body to cover her with his weight. To glory in feeling all of her at once.

She planted her feet against the blanket and pressed upward again as he moved his finger within her, prompting him to move above her, soothing her rising need with the press of his body. He kissed her deeply, his tongue tangling with hers in rhythm with his hands, and when she subsided, he eased another long finger alongside the first. A rush of heat and desire ripped into his gut at the scalding heat of her passage as it closed tightly around his fingers. He tried to move them slightly, to stretch her just a little bit more, so she would be ready for him.

Tressa let out a gloriously breathy moan and her hips rose off the ground with the gentle pulse of his fingers. She was so bloody close, and he concentrated on grazing his thumb every so lightly against the sensitive nub shielded by her sweet flesh. She arched wildly one last time and he swallowed her cry as her climax shuddered through her.

Matthew kissed her again and slowly withdrew his hands from her body. She was glorious. He lay next to her and took pleasure watching what little he could see of her face as she drifted on the ebbing tide of her ecstasy.

Her shattered breathing began to slow and ease, gradually returning toward normal, but he wasn't done with her yet. Not by a long, long shot. Fate had been both persistent and kind in delivering her to him, and he was damn well going to make the most of the opportunity.

Matthew wanted her so badly he ached. For her, this long, tall drink of girl in his arms, and he wanted to make the most of the precious time he had with her. The devil only knew what might come of his rapidly changing plans—the plans he didn't yet know if he could bring to fruition.

But she was here, now, and they were together, and she was gloriously naked. And she was his and no one else's.

He kissed her again, and again his hands delved into the silky glory of her hair, sliding across his palms. He meant to kiss her lightly, to give her time to recover, but she stirred and nuzzled delightfully at his throat, and his lust and his cock rose with each supple stir of her body, every subtle friction of her skin against his.

Merciless devil, but he couldn't wait another moment to have her.

He kissed her more deeply as he settled firmly between her legs, pushing her legs wide with his knees, as he guided himself into her welcoming flesh.

"Easy. Slowly, love," he whispered, though there was nothing easy about it—he was nothing but barely controlled impulse.

He gave in to the need to taste her, taking her nipple into his mouth in a way that made her throw her head back and gasp into the night.

And damned if he wasn't smiling, too. His hand replaced

his mouth at her breast when Tressa pulled his mouth up to hers, kissing him back, sliding her tongue with his as if she wanted the taste, and the smell and the feel of him around her just as much as he wanted her.

Her body began to move in response to his, her hips shifting languorously beneath him. He pressed up higher on his arms, taking his weight off her, and flexed his hip muscles against her.

"Oh, better, Kent." She breathed his name as if it were a prayer. "Better still."

Tressa arched into him, and he lowered his head to her breast, suckling her in time with the pulse of his body into her center. She closed her eyes and ran her hands up his arms, kneading the bunched muscles there and across his chest, making him heedless and happy, drunk on her delirious bliss.

"Do that again."

"This?" She ran her hands across his chest again, slower this time, her fingers tracing over his nipples in imitation of the way he had touched hers. "Do you like that?"

"Aye." He rose higher upon his knees, pulling her tight against him before he let go of her hips, and molded his hands to cup her breasts. He flicked the tight peaks with his callused thumbs.

A carnal sound of encouragement and need broke from her mouth as her eyes crashed shut.

He felt it too, the crashing wave of pleasure pooling deep into his belly. His breath began to saw in and out of his chest, and his vision began to narrow until there was nothing else but her. Her beauty. Her body. Her bliss.

He wanted to hold her again, to feel her energy, the heat of her desire, so he ran his hands down over her hips and around to her bottom, tracing the swift curve of her sweet arse with his palms, kneading her flesh as he rose up upon his knees. He surged into her, stronger and stronger, feeding the need, stoking the fiery heat that built where their bodies touched.

Matthew felt her slipping away, losing herself to the inexorable whirl of sensations.

She clutched at his arms, trying to anchor herself against the relentless onslaught of pressure and pleasure, even as she planted her feet flat against the blanket and angled her body higher.

The pleasure was so intense it was almost pain, almost a burden to hold back. Matthew felt his coat beside her head, and stuffed it under her bottom, leveraging her up.

She made a sound of appreciative approval, and pushed her thighs higher, clutching at him with her thighs. And in answer, he drove the breath from both of their lungs with the simple efficacy of lifting her legs flat against his chest.

And there she was, all sinuous passion and beauty before him. "This, Teague. This is best." All feeling, all sensation, all emotion converged into the bone deep feeling of ecstasy. "You are best."

CHAPTER 19

THE SHARP, aching pleasure bolted back through Tressa. She heard a low keening moan and knew it came from her, that it was a sound of approval as much as distress, because it felt so good, too good—a pleasure so intense she could not escape it.

But Matthew was a vision of power and male beauty. She watched his hands round to her hips and pull her up high against him. She felt a jolt of such intense, joyous pleasure streak through her, and something inside, some last vestige of reason or restraint came untethered and ran riot. Some heady, insistent, intoxicating mixture of greed and joy that rose higher with each escalating thrust.

She watched him, rising above her with such intensity that her heart felt joined to his. She felt him, apart from her and yet in her all at the same time, and she knew in that instant what it meant to be undone—to let go of every last tie to reason and give way to the glorious physical wash of upending emotion that shot through her.

She closed her eyes and felt him stroke his hand down her

belly, into the thatch of curls crowning her body where they were joined. He teased his fingers through the hair, then slipped his fingers lower, ever so slightly lower, to the sensitive engorged flesh below.

Tressa cried out again. It was too much and not enough all at the same time. She had to move, to do more. To find the last drop of ecstasy that was just out of reach. And Matthew wanted to find it too—he pulled her back hard against him, holding her hips still against him as he surged inside her.

He held her so—so that something changed and sharpened, and it felt so, so good, so incredibly pleasurable that Tressa felt as if she was dissolving into a hundred different pieces of bliss.

But instead of dissolving, she shattered. Falling to a hundred thousand pieces of exquisite pleasure. And he clasped his mouth to hers just as she screamed.

Pink and grey dawn slanted under the edge of the dory and pierced his eyelids.

Damn his eyes, was it actually morning? How had he slept through the cold and the storm? Well, he *had* been occupied with the warm bundle of contradictions spooned against him under the haphazard heapings of clothes and cloak.

The warm bundle of contradictions who was awake and looking at him with an embarrassed sort of happy satisfaction.

He smiled, reaching out to gather her to him. "Morning, sweet Teague."

"Hello, my captain." Her smile was everything in his world.

Except that they were far from the world they needed to

return to. "Let us bestir ourselves so I can take my turn at saving us this morning."

"About time." She sorted through the heap of clothes covering them. "Heavens, but it's cold."

Matthew peered out into the unusually bright morning and hastened to dress himself so he could find what lay outside their cozy shelter. "The storm brought a heavy frost—no, it's ice."

While they had been heating themselves with love, the storm had brought a rime of ice that coated the shoreline in a brittle casing. "At least it should keep the soldiers in their barracks."

Tressa followed him out. "Tide's on the rise." Her words curled into wisps in the cold air over her head. "I think we should take the blanket, and head across the dunes for the other boat. It has some food—apples and cheese and ale—although they might be frozen."

"Teague, how am I to take my turn to save us, if you will keep using that superior brain of yours?" But he carefully stowed the pistol in his belt, folded up the blanket and slung it across his body and under his belt before he took her hand. "Though I *am* following your superior plan, I will insist on the navigation—this way."

He led them at a slow run, lest anyone from the fort be raking the coast with a spyglass looking for anything amiss. If they did see them, Matthew hoped they would only see two lovers out for a morning tryst.

And to lend veracity to his imagined scenario, he stopped and kissed her—a lovely soft, sighing kiss of sweet morning desire. "I cannot wait to get you on the other side of this channel, Teague, and all to myself in a comfortable, warm bed."

"Then we had better keep moving if we're to make it that far, Captain."

It was the work of another thirteen minutes to locate the boat and drag it across the beach to where the high tide was cresting. "Get in before you get your feet wet, Teague. And that's an order."

"Aye, aye, Captain." Tressa hopped nimbly over the low rail, muttering, "I'd much rather take the tiller and captain the boat than try to captain you."

"You do that," Matthew growled, following her into the boat before the water could get higher than his boots—after last night's frigid dunking Matthew was loath to get that wet and cold again. A sailor was far more likely to perish from exposure than he was from a cannonball.

But Tressa kept him from getting wet by her efficient competence—she already had the mast stepped and the sail filling with wind by the time he was seated in the stern-sheets. All he had to do was take up the tiller and head them straight into the cold, blue-grey waves.

"We'll head straight for Dover and see what we can get from there—I don't fancy sailing down channel in an open boat in this weather." The worst of the storm had left its icy rime on the coast, but the sky was still an ominous bone-cold grey—packed tight with brooding clouds—and the wind blew as if it had come straight from the frozen coast of Norway.

"Aye." Tressa gathered the edges of her cloak tighter against the chill.

"Come sit with me. We'll make ourselves merry and warm."

She readily cuddled up tight, but she was not the sort of lass who could be idle. "Shift yourself for a moment, I want to get a glass out from under the seat."

She lifted the hinged counter and rummaged around until she extracted a spyglass and another stout woolen blanket. "Wrap our legs in this."

But Matthew did not take her advice to wrap up, for his attention was taken up with a sleek sloop, bearing down from the west, close-hauled on the larboard tack—something about it alarmed his instinct enough to make him alter his own course so he would not cross its bow.

But the sloop promptly changed course as well.

"Do you see that sloop?" Tressa's instincts seemed to be equally alarmed—he reckoned the sloop was the reason she had fetched the spyglass, which she now trained on the approaching vessel. "Matthew, I think they're trying to—" She passed him the glass and took the tiller in his stead. "I think they're trying to hail us."

Matthew found the vessel clearly in the glass, raking her bow before he moved to the figure at the rail. "God's balls. It's my bloody interfering sister. And her bloody tattling husband."

"Sally Kent?" Tressa snatched back the glass.

"Sally Kent Colyear," Matthew clarified, "lest you two get any ideas about wandering off to conquer the seas—not that I doubt your ability to do so." Indeed, if Teague and his sister got together, he shuddered to think of the consequences.

But on the other hand—they were bound to be so successful, he and Col would likely never have to work another day in their lives. They could keep the navy as a hobby.

With that particularly idiotic, but amusing, idea winching about his brain, Matthew changed course to fall in with the sloop, and marveled at how lucky he really was. He had always admired how sympathetic Sally and Col were to each other—how their marriage was founded upon principles of respect and admiration. He had envied them.

Envied them but never hoped to join them. He had thought his sister too unique, too odd. It was too strange to think that there could ever be another lass as ambitious and competent and clever in all the world.

But here she was, nestled next to him in an open boat on the English Channel at the tail end of a December gale. He'd be a fool if he didn't marry her straightaway.

And though Matthew Kent knew himself to be many things, he was no fool.

CHAPTER 20

"YOU'LL LIKE Cliff House, I hope."

Tressa was too busy working to calm her nerves at meeting Sally Kent to wonder what had prompted that particularly errant comment. "I'm sure it's lovely."

She was only slightly less anxious about meeting Matthew's family—after a night of sleeping rough in, and out, of her own clothes—than she had been in Falmouth. But as this meeting appeared unavoidable—and frankly welcome, for she had much rather be tucked up out of the wind on the sloop than freeze in her clammy cloak—Tressa tried to push aside the uneasy feeling swirling in the pit of her belly.

"Sal had the run of the place for a while, and may again, though Grace certainly likes to have her own way best."

"Don't we all," Tressa murmured. She was also concerned about what Sally Kent's husband, Captain Colyear, might make of her after his first erroneous impression.

But Matthew was still going merrily on. "Grace has no family of her own, you see, so she rather likes having everyone there. She'll be glad enough of Sally's company, now that she'll be home, but she won't mind at all your coming to live with them."

"Live with them. Why should I live with them?" She sounded like a looby, echoing his words. She would go to Cliff House, of course, to convince Sally Colyear and Lady Grace Kent, and whomever else she might, to help finance a cargo and perhaps even the ship that Tressa eventually wanted for her own.

"All the wives have done it at one time or another."

Everything within her strangled to a stop—even her heart seemed to stutter still.

"Funny how when we were young the house was so full of boys," he went on. "Sally excepting, of course. And now Cliff House is entirely full of women—Grace and Owen have only girls, like your family."

Tressa felt like she must not have attended him properly—she could not make sense of this information. The possibility of what he was saying was too big, too important for her to have missed.

Half a cable's length away, the sloop hove to, lying into the wind so the smaller boat could approach them.

It was now or never. "Kent. Are you by some small mischance proposing to me?"

Matthew laughed in that merry, mischievous way of his—as if nothing could possibly be wrong. "I suppose I am, though we've gone a bit far out of range for a proposal. I've no idea how to manage it, for there's no time for the banns to be read in the traditional manner, and I've neither the time nor the money to waste to either go to Doctor's Commons and make my plea or pay to get a bishop in my pocket. I don't suppose you know anything about a common license, do you, being the daughter of a vicar."

"Kent. Shut up."

"Not that I'm poor—I suppose I ought to have told you

that I've made a respectable enough fortune that we can afford to marry straightaway."

"Kent. For the love of God, please shut up."

Mercifully, he did so. But now he was staring at her. "Do you mean to refuse me?"

"No, actually, I don't. But I had rather you'd actually *asked* first." She meant for them to hash it out properly, betwixt the two of them, and no one else, to come to a right agreement. "So instead, I'll ask you. Matthew Aloysius Kent—"

"How in bloody hell did you know that?"

She tucked her chin down and gave him her most knowing smile. "My darling Captain, don't you know? I know everything."

"God's balls." His face clouded and cleared in such rapid succession she could not prepare for what he said next. "Then you know I can't read."

Tressa felt as if the wind had been knocked clean out of her—the cold air hurt to breathe. But at the same time, everything made sense—from his reliance on her knowledge of the smuggling records to his asking her to read the map.

"You didn't know." He closed his eyes and tipped his face skyward as if he wished he could call the words back. But there was no going back on such a revelation. "I mean, I can read, a little. A very little. It's devilish difficult. Bloody damn hard."

"How did you get on as a midshipman, or pass your lieutenancy exams?"

"Col and Sally—they tutored and hectored me through for the lieutenancy somehow, damned if they didn't. And the rest I simply memorized through sheer force of will. And when I'm aboard ship, I've a clerk and lieutenants to dictate my reports to. That's why I left Bocka Morrow—I needed to make my report from home. Grace wrote it all out for me from my dictation."

"And the incident in Norway?" She had never learned the exact details of the incident that had seen him stripped of his command—the newspapers that carried the Admiralty dispatches referred only to an unsuccessful on-shore assault.

He shook his head, as if in doing so he might clear the whole of the bad memory from his brain. "My lieutenant was down with a fever, and I couldn't read the damned orders—it was in a hand so crabbed and scrawled it might as well have been in Norwegian for all I could tell. So, I acted without them."

"I see." What she also saw was that Matthew had put the bow of the dory into the wind so they were luffing, bobbing on the waves while the passengers on the sloop stood by impatiently. "Well then, we'd best get aboard."

His hand clenched on the tiller. "Teague—Tressa. I need your answer."

"No," she said, because she wasn't quite ready to let him off the metaphorical hook without some teasing. "It is you who haven't given *me* your answer. After all, I am the one who proposed properly."

"Do you still want me?"

"Do you still love me?"

He took her hand. "I may be nearly illiterate, but I am not stupid." He kissed her palm. "Of course, I love you. With all that I am, and with all that I hope to be with you by my side."

"Then, my dear Captain Kent, I think that you have courage and confidence and charm enough to make me want to marry you. And you had better marry me, for I don't know another woman who could want so badly to be your equal."

The look on this face—the relief and excitement and sheer, unadulterated happiness—made her own eyes swim with joy. "Devil take me, Teague, I wouldn't have you any other way. You, Tressa Teague, are without a doubt my fortune and my treasure."

Tressa closed her eyes and let go of reason and let herself feel. She felt his kiss draw her into the enchanted dreamland that existed between waking and sleep, where every thought gave way to a hundred feelings, and every feeling dissolved into a hundred more sensations of sensual satisfaction.

A satisfaction that danced over the surface of her skin, whirling through her blood, skipping its way deep into her bones. Beneath the cover of her cloak and the confines of her clothes, her body grew restless—dissatisfied by the constraints of fabric and fashion. Her breasts grew sensitive and tender, longing for a different kind of touch.

"You had better marry me quickly, Kent. For I shall become quite the fallen woman if you do not."

He laughed until tears formed in the corner of his eyes. "Devil take me, Tressa my love, if that doesn't sound entirely promising."

A shout came from the sloop. "Did she say yes?"

Matthew's eves were all for Tressa even as he shouted back, "Aye, damn your interfering eyes, she did."

"Huzzah!" At the rail of the sloop, Sally Kent cheered in open delight. "Then my dear friend Tressa, let me be the first to wish you happy. You shall and must be a Christmastide bride, for no one else on this blue Earth could be such a match for my charming, mischievous, darling brother."

CHAPTER 21

THE FRENCH had a word for it, of course, being the French and the damned enemy, though they were only a day's sail away across the Channel. The *coup de foudre*, they called it—the stroke of lightning, the moment of force when everything changed.

And everything changed again the glorious Christmastide day that long, tall Tressa Teague strode out of the vicarage and down the holly and ivy-clad aisle of St. David's Church, and made an honest man out of him in the presence of both her family and his.

All his family, brothers and sisters and husbands and wives attended. Even Richard, who seemed a tad put out not to be asked to conduct the nuptials himself. Yet as his beloved mentor, the Reverend Teague, was conducting the service, he demurred with only the faintest hint of frustration.

They married on Christmas Eve, at the ungodly and unseemly hour of eight o'clock in the morning, as the Reverend Teague was needed elsewhere in the town or countryside or at Castle Keyvnor to marry some other couples, who could not possibly be as happy or as well-suited as Tressa and Matthew.

But his bride's joy was made complete by marrying at home, in the traditional manner, after the banns had been read on three successive Sundays, with all her family there, with her dear, awkward, uncomfortable, but determinedly loyal friend Felicity standing by the altar her as bridesmaid, and her father conducting the solemn service that joined them in wedded bliss.

There was, in fact so much wedded bliss in Bocka Morrow that Christmastide, that the tiny village's reputation for being the best place to find true love was already beginning to spread beyond the borders of Cornwall—even Richard spoke interestingly of perhaps taking up the curacy, there—and into the wider world.

And that was where Matthew was going—back into the wide blue world. With her by his side. Just as soon as she married him.

And she got to show him off at the Yule Ball.

And so, he tugged his best dress uniform into place, and stood in nave of St. David's Church before the altar, instead of up on the parapet of the belfry where Tressa had asked that they be married—the vicar was a liberal man, but not even he would stretch his scruples that far.

Instead, the vicar looked over the top of his spectacles and down the length of his nose and began. "Wilt thou, Matthew Aloysius Kent—"

"Aloysius," she muttered beside him. "It has a ring to it. Perhaps I should start calling you—"

"You will not," Matthew muttered back. And then to the nonplussed vicar he said, "I will indeed, Reverend Teague, have this darling, difficult woman to my wedded wife, to live together after God's ordinance in the holy estate of matrimony. I will love her, comfort her, honor and keep her in sickness and in health, and, forsaking all others, keep only unto her, so long as we both shall live."

"Oh, well done, Aloysius," his bride-in-progress murmured.

"Don't count your broadsides before they're fired, Teague. You're next."

"If you two wouldn't mind." The Reverend Teague looked over the top of his spectacles, and down the impressive length of his nose with decided annoyance. "Wilt thou, Tressa Trinity Teague—"

She shot Matthew a triumphant look.

"Wilt thou have this man to thy wedded husband, to live together after God's ordinance in the holy estate of matrimony. To love him, comfort him, honor, obey, and keep him in sickness and in health, and, forsaking all others, keep only unto him, so long as ye both shall live?"

"Aye. Indeed, I will."

The relief that soared through his blood must have been joy—joy that at last, all was right with the world, and there was nothing he could not do with her by his side, even escort her to the bloody Yule Ball at Castle Keyvnor later that night.

He would spend the time in the ballroom happily planning his campaign for what he would do with her later that night, and how they would celebrate long into Christmas morning.

He had been struck by lightning, and damned if it wasn't the pleasantest thing.

Damned if he didn't have the devil's own luck.

THANK YOU FOR READING

Thank you for reading *The Devil's Own Luck*. I hope you'll take a few minutes out of your day to review this book – your honest opinion is much appreciated. Reviews help introduce readers to new authors they wouldn't otherwise meet.

To keep up to date on Elizabeth's books, sign up for her newsletter and get exclusive excerpts, contests, and more at her WEBSITE.

Please turn the page for an exciting excerpt from Elizabeth Essex's First Reckless Brides novel

ALMOST A SCANDAL,

the story of Matthew's sister Sally Kent, and her adventurous time aboard *HMS Audacious.*

ALMOST A SCANDAL

Portsmouth, England
Autumn 1805

IT WASN'T THE FIRST TIME Sally Kent had donned a worn, hand-me-down uniform from one of her brothers' sea chests, but it was the first time it had felt so completely, perfectly right.

She had always been tall and spare, strong for a girl, but dressed in the uniform of His Majesty's Royal Navy, she felt more than strong. She felt powerful.

Powerful enough to ignore the voice of conscience thundering in her ear, telling her she needed to stay quietly on land and learn to be a young lady. Powerful enough to face down the potential scandal. Powerful enough to abandon her younger brother to his chosen fate.

Because her brother Richard had rejected all claims to duty and honor. He had forsaken his family. He wasn't coming back.

That morning, the very morning he was to have worn his uniform and boarded His Majesty's Ship *Audacious* with all the other candidates for midshipmen, he had disappeared, gone as if he had been swallowed whole by the heavy, obliterating rain.

Richard had left her, quite literally, holding his bag.

And she was going to use it.

Sally closed her mind to the insistent whispering of her conscience, wrapped her breasts in cotton strapping, and put on every single piece of that uniform, from the faded blue midshipman's coat and white breeches, down to the black buckled shoes.

She ignored the uneven pounding of her heart, and took a scissors to her hair. She jammed the dark beaver hat low over her eyes, clattered down the narrow stairs and out of the inn.

She swallowed the sharp edges of her fear, crossed the wet cobbles, and took her brother's place in the rain at the sally port on Portsmouth's rain-drenched quay.

"Richard Kent."

A lieutenant glared at her from under the dripping brim of his cocked hat—an irate lieutenant, his eyes glittering like a flash of black powder.

He stood in the stern of a ship's boat, impervious to the filthy weather and the rise and fall of the vessel tossing fitfully beneath him. The sharp vertical lines of the scowl between his dark brows could have scraped barnacles off a hull, but his low voice was incongruously smooth.

"This is His Majesty's Royal Navy, Kent, not a damned church fête. We're not going to issue you a bloody invitation."

Sally jerked her chin into her collar to hide beneath the dark brim of her hat. She would have known that deep, laconic voice anywhere, even over the pounding din of the rain.

David St. Vincent Colyear.

But would he know her?

He had been eighteen years old and on the verge of taking his lieutenant's exam the last time she had seen him, the summer her brother Matthew had brought him home to Falmouth.

Col, they had called him. Six years ago, he had been long and lean, but by God, clad in the endless fall of his gray sea cloak, he was a leviathan now. A great oaken mast of a man looming up from the waist of the small boat.

A man grown. A man whose jaw looked as sharp as an axe blade and whose piercing eyes, the color of green chalcedony stone, were just as hard and impenetrable.

Sally pushed her voice deeper. "Aye, sir," she answered. "I'm Richard Kent."

"I know." Col's voice was low and dangerously soft—disconcerting in such a hard-looking man. "Now get in the bloody boat."

ABOUT THE AUTHOR

ELIZABETH ESSEX is a *USA Today* bestselling author of over twenty critically acclaimed historical romances, including the Reckless Brides and Highland Brides series.

Her books have been nominated for numerous awards, including the Gayle Wilson Award of Excellence, the Romantic Times Reviewers' Choice and Seal of Excellence Awards, and RWA's prestigious RITA Award. The Reckless Brides Series has also made Top-Ten lists from Romantic Times, The Romance Reviews and Affaire de Coeur Magazine, and every book in the series was awarded Desert Isle Keeper status at All About Romance. Her fifth book, A BREATH OF SCANDAL, was named Best Historical in the Reader's Crown 2013.

When not rereading Jane Austen, mucking about in her garden, walking her beloved dogs, Ghillie and Brogue, or simply messing about with boats, Elizabeth can be always be found with her laptop, making up stories about heroes and heroines who live far more exciting lives than she.

It wasn't always so. Long before she ever set pen to paper, Elizabeth graduated from Hollins College with a BA in Classics and Art History, and then earned her MA in Nautical Archaeology from Texas A&M University. While she loved the academic life of an underwater archaeologist, she has found her true calling writing lush, lyrical historical romance full of mystery, passion, daring and adventure.

Elizabeth lives in Texas with her husband, the Indispensable Mr. Essex, and her active and exuberant family in an old house filled to the brim with books.

Elizabeth loves to hear from readers, so please feel free to contact her at the following places:

ALSO BY ELIZABETH ESSEX

Reckless Brides

Almost a Scandal

A Breath of Scandal

After the Scandal

A Scandal to Remember

The Scandal Before Christmas (novella)

A Lady's Gift for Scandal (holiday novella)

The Difference One Duke Makes (novella)

She Walks in Scandal (novella in *A Midsummer Night's Romance* Anthology)

Highland Brides

Mad for Love (long novella)

Mad About the Marquess

A Fine Madness

Mad, Plaid and Dangerous to Marry

Mad Dogs and Englishwomen (Coming soon!)

Dartmouth Brides

The Pursuit of Pleasure

A Sense of Sin

The Danger of Desire

The Dartmouth Brides Boxed Set (with holiday novella "*Up on the Rooftops*")

The Kent Brothers Chronicles

Between the Devil & the Deep Blue Sea ~ and ~ The Devil's Own Luck

To keep up to date on new releases and events, sign up for Elizabeth's newsletter and get exclusive excerpts, contests, and more

http://www.elizabethessex.com

I also hope you'll take a few minutes out of your day to review this book – your honest opinion is much appreciated. Reviews help introduce readers to new authors they wouldn't otherwise meet.

Printed in Dunstable, United Kingdom